PENGUIN CRIME FICTION
SILENT KNIVES

Laurence Gough has written plays for Canadian
radio and is at work on another Willow and Parker
novel. He lives with his wife and children in
Vancouver, Canada.

SILENT KNIVES

LAURENCE GOUGH

PENGUIN BOOKS

PENGUIN BOOKS
Published by the Penguin Group
Viking Penguin, a division of Penguin Books USA Inc.,
40 West 23rd Street, New York, New York 10010, U.S.A.
Penguin Books Ltd, 27 Wrights Lane, London W8 5TZ, England
Penguin Books Australia Ltd, Ringwood, Victoria, Australia
Penguin Books Canada Ltd, 2801 John Street, Markham, Ontario, Canada L3R 1B4
Penguin Books (N.Z.) Ltd, 182–190 Wairau Road, Auckland 10, New Zealand

Penguin Books Ltd, Registered Offices: Harmondsworth, Middlesex, England

First published in Great Britain under the title *Death on a No. 8 Hook* by Victor
Gollancz Limited, 1988
First published in the United States of America by St. Martin's Press, 1988
Reprinted by arrangement with St. Martin's Press
Published in Penguin Books 1990

10 9 8 7 6 5 4 3 2 1

LIBRARY OF CONGRESS CATALOGING IN PUBLICATION DATA
Gough, Laurence.
    Silent knives / Laurence Gough.
        p.   cm.
    ISBN 0 14 01.2189 7
    I. Title.
    [PR9199.3.G652S5   1990]
    813'.54—dc20   89-29941

Printed in the United States of America

This one is for my mother

The death of the horse is the
life of the crow.
　　　　　　　– Newfoundland
　　　　　　　　proverb

1

The call Mannie had been waiting for all his adult life came late on a Tuesday morning.

He was brunching, reading the sports section of the morning rag and pushing a few last soggy flakes of Sugar Crisps around the bowl. When the phone rang he was so startled that he dropped his spoon, splattering milk across the front of his imitation silk dressing-gown.

The gown was bright red with angry gold dragons all over it. The right pocket sagged under the weight of an Italian switchblade. Mannie was very much into knives. They were like American Express cards to him. He never left home without one.

It was a collect call, from Los Angeles. Mannie didn't ask who wanted to speak to him. He accepted the charges without hesitation.

The guy on the other end of the line did a pretty fair Donald Duck. His voice was wet, explosive, full of repressed anger.

"Donald," said Mannie, "How's it going?"

There was a pause. Then a sudden burst of spittle. "This is Daffy, asshole."

Mannie tried to keep it light. "You shouldn't talk duck and use that kind of language," he said. "If Walt could hear you, he'd roll over in his grave."

"Fuck Walt."

There was a long silence, a silence that stretched into minutes. Mannie had left his cigarettes on the kitchen table. His lungs ached. He listened to the faint hiss and moan of seventeen hundred miles of static. Another minute dragged by. He took the knife out of his pocket and pressed the chrome button mounted in the handle. The blade flicked out, locked into place. Mannie used the razor edge to peel thin strips of plastic from the telephone cord. Finally he lost patience and said, "You still there, Daffy?"

7

"Why, you busy?"

"Depends what you've got in mind," said Mannie.

"I was thinking about snapping my fingers and watching you jump!" the duck squawked angrily. It raised its voice a little. "Is there any more champagne around here, or what?"

Mannie heard the sound of liquid fizzing from a bottle.

"Just to the brim," said Felix Newton in his normal tone of voice. "Thanks, baby. You're a doll."

"What's the occasion?" said Mannie, "You finally graduate from the Berlitz School of Duck?"

"I been polishing my act all day. My fucking throat is killing me. But at least I think I'm getting somewhere, making some progress. Then you come waltzing into my life. Christ, anybody can do a fucking Donald!"

"If you were about seventeen hundred miles closer, you could lean over and cry on my shoulder."

"Listen," said Felix, "if I want some laughs outta you, chum, I'll buy you a baggy black and white check suit and a big red plastic nose. Understand?"

"Sure," said Mannie, subdued.

There was a sound like miniature thunder. Felix had a place on the ocean just south of Laguna Beach. Mannie had never been there, but he had a mental picture. He imagined Felix Newton's squat blunt fingers drumming on the white-painted metal of a patio tabletop, a vein pulsing ominously in the side of his neck. Maybe turning to glare at somebody walking by.

"Mannie," said Felix, "the reason I called is because there's a little something I want you to do for me."

"Like what?"

"There's some people I want killed."

Mannie swallowed noisily.

"You still there, or have you gone and fainted dead away on me?"

"Should we be talking about this kind of stuff on the phone?"

"Sure. Why not?"

"Aren't you worried somebody might be listening in?"

"Like who?"

"Jeez, how should I know?"

Felix grunted derisively. "I'm clean at my end, and nobody gives a shit about you, Mannie. You keep living like a rabbit,

8

probably nobody ever will." Felix's voice suddenly became very quiet. "Hold on a minute, I'll be right back."

Mannie heard a noise that must have been the phone hitting the table. Indecipherable whispered fragments of conversation. A woman giggling. Felix shouting. A shrapnel burst of laughter, high-pitched and verging on hysteria. A meaty thud.

Silence.

"Tell me something," said Felix, "What's the weather like up there in Canada?"

"I don't know." Mannie hadn't looked outside since he'd got up. "You want me to check?"

"It's in the high eighties down here. We got a nice breeze coming in off the water. No smog. A sky so blue you'd think the colour had just been invented." Felix had his breathing under control now. He cleared his throat. "You ought to fly down for a visit one of these days. I think you'd like it. In fact, I think you'd fit right in."

"Terrific," said Mannie.

"But first of all, there's these three kids I want you to take care of for me. Does three grand each plus expenses sound pretty good?"

"Five's the going rate."

"Click," said Felix. "That was the sound of me hanging up. You want to hear it again, or you want to take the money and run?"

"American?"

"What?"

"American money, Felix?"

"You think I'd deal in that useless Canadian shit?"

"No, I guess not."

"It has to be done real quiet, Mannie. No muss and absolutely no fuss. Low profile. I'm gonna send Junior around to give you a hand with the groundwork."

"You don't have to do that," said Mannie quickly.

"Oh yes I do. He'll be in touch. Expect him when he gets there. You got a pencil and a piece of paper?"

"Just a minute," said Mannie. He had a pad and a Bic pen sitting right there in front of him, but Felix had no way of knowing that. And for some reason the idea of keeping Felix

9

waiting appealed to Mannie. He went over to the kitchen table and got his cigarettes, lit up and came back to the phone.

"Go ahead, shoot."

"Take down these names," said Felix. "Make sure you get the spelling right because this is important to me and I don't want any mistakes."

"Okay," said Mannie. He did a little scribbling to make sure the pen worked. Felix gave him the names of the three kids he wanted killed. Mannie wrote laboriously, in clumsy block letters, his narrow face pinched and shrunken with the force of his concentration. As soon as he was sure that Mannie had it all down on paper, Felix hung up.

2

The alarm-clock had been made in Yugoslavia. It was fire-engine red and had a big moon face of white enamel. The numerals were Roman, thick and black. The clock had two shiny brass bells on top, tilted at an angle to each other. Between the bells stood a functional hammer, also of brass. When the alarm went off, the jangling of the bells was impossible to ignore.

Detective Jack Willows opened his eyes and saw the clock jabbering and shuddering towards him, vibrating its way across the night table as if it had a life of its own. He reached out and shut the machine off.

Silence descended.

It was Friday morning, five a.m. The three-day weekend he'd finally managed to squeeze out of Superintendent Bradley was underway at last.

Willows showered, shaved quickly, and got dressed. He made toast and drank two cups of coffee, filled his thermos with the rest of the pot. By a quarter past six he was on the Upper Levels highway, heading west. Vancouver was behind and below him. On his right stood sheer walls of orange and brown rock that had been blasted out of the flank of the mountain. To his left the ocean gleamed bright as tinfoil under the early morning sun.

At Horseshoe Bay, twenty miles out of town, the highway abruptly narrowed to single lanes. Willows held his Oldsmobile to a steady forty miles an hour, keeping well over to his side of the yellow line as he drove through the endless sharp turns, blind corners. Traffic was light, most of it commuters heading towards the city. Howe Sound lay quietly in the shade of the mountains, the ocean dark green and the scattered islands a pale, greyish-blue.

This was Willows' first holiday in months. He needed badly to get away from things, and he knew it.

Dutifully, he made a point of enjoying the scenery.

Forty miles out of Vancouver, he drove past the small town of Squamish. The ocean here at the head of the Sound was a sickly yellow colour, and the air stank of rotten eggs. There was a rumour that a local woman had died from eating mercury-contaminated shellfish. So far the government had done nothing, and the nearby pulpmills continued to spew out tons of pollutants a day. Willows rolled up his window. He put his foot down on the gas and kept it there until he had left the stench far behind.

He drove for another half-hour, and then braked hard and turned off the highway, down a gravel logging road cut through the trees. The road was hard-packed and steeply cambered to shed the spring rains. There were potholes everywhere, and some bad washboarding. Willows slowed down, and then slowed down some more. Fifty yards in from the highway the road curved sharply off to the left. Just beyond the curve there was a white-painted gatehouse with a shingled roof.

Willows drove past the gatehouse and pulled over to the side of the road. He turned off the Oldsmobile's engine, and got out of the car.

The watchman waited until most of the dust had settled before showing himself. When he slid open the gatehouse door, Willows heard a snatch of calypso music. Then the door slid shut with a bang.

The watchman was in his late fifties, with dark brown hair and a heavy, weathered face. He was wearing a green uniform with a Sam Browne belt. Above his heart a shiny outsized badge was pinned to his shirt. He held a peaked cap loosely in his hands. The cap had another big badge on it. The watchman put the cap on his head, pulling the brim down low. As he walked towards the Oldsmobile, Willows noticed that his left foot was turned slightly inward and that the leg didn't bend at the knee.

The watchman stopped beside the rear bumper of the car. He ran his hand lightly over the gently curving slope of the metal, used the ball of a calloused thumb to rub dust from the thick, ruby-red glass of the rear light. He gave Willows a quick, shy smile. "About a forty-three, is she?"

"On the nose," said Willows.

"Original paint, by the look of her. Big straight eight engine?"

"That's right."

"How's the mileage, if you don't mind me askin'?"

"Terrible," admitted Willows.

The watchman gave him another quick grin. He showed teeth this time, and his face went lopsided with the effort. Willows saw that there was scar tissue all down the left side, a flow of slick white flesh from eye socket to jawline.

"Back when this here vehicle was made," the watchman said, "gas cost what, about a dime a gallon? Nobody I knew ever thought about or cared where the damn stuff came from. Or how much of it was left. Times sure have changed, haven't they?"

"Yes indeed," said Willows amiably.

The watchman took another step forward and leaned to peer through the rear window. He eyed Willows' small pack, his hip waders, the dark, burnished leather of his rod case. "Planning to do a little fishin'?"

Willows nodded. "Thought I'd try a few of the small creeks."

"Nothing much in the big river at this time of the year."

"I know."

"Stayin' long?"

"I'll be out by noon on Sunday," said Willows. He wasn't used to being questioned. It took him an effort not to show his impatience.

"Headed anywhere in particular?"

"Wherever there's fish."

"Or you think there might be, eh?"

The watchman chuckled, pleased with his joke. He was still peering myopically through the rear window, his forearm resting on the glass. "Must be brand-new upholstery in there, by the look of it."

"Had it done this spring."

"Expensive?"

"Let's just say it cost too much, and leave it at that."

The watchman nodded, and pushed away from the car. Willows belatedly realized that the man had been covertly studying his reflection in the car mirror. Probably it was a trick he'd learned watching cops and robbers on TV.

"Camped up in this neck of the woods before, have you?"

"Not for a couple of years."

"Well, she's just as much a wilderness now as she was then. People still get lost real frequent, and it still costs the company a fortune to go lookin' for them. Whether they ever get found, or not."

Willows repressed a smile. "I'll keep that in mind, thank you."

"And watch out for them damn loggin' trucks. Those buggers weigh ten tons apiece. Most of the time they couldn't stop for you even if they wanted to."

"I'll remember."

The watchman rubbed his hands together, scrubbing away the dust he'd picked up from the Oldsmobile. "One more thing," he said, "before you go."

"What's that?" said Willows shortly.

"Enjoy yourself, you hear!"

Now it was Willows' turn to smile.

The watchman waited until the Oldsmobile was a long way down the road before he turned and walked stiffly back to the gatehouse. Inside, he licked the stub of a pencil and wrote the date and exact time in his log, and then the year and make and licence number of Willows' car. Below that he noted Willows' stated intention to leave no later than noon the following Sunday. When he had finished writing, he took off his cap and tossed it down on his desk.

Then he sat down in his wooden chair, on the plump crocheted cushion which his wife had made for him, and turned up the volume on his radio.

Willows drove cautiously, keeping the Oldsmobile under twenty miles an hour. On either side of the road, the trees and underbrush had been cut back fifteen feet to reduce the risk of fire caused by exhaust sparks or carelessly handled cigarettes. Beyond this narrow strip of waste ground there was a mix of second-growth fir and cedar, the spreading branches thickly coated with a fine white dust. On both sides of the road, high up, there were huge brown patches, each encompassing several square miles, where the mountains had been clear-cut and the foliage stripped right down to the bare earth.

During the rest of that Friday morning, Willows pulled over

to the side of the road several times to make exploratory forays into the woods. Without fail, the stream that had caught his interest gradually dwindled in size until it was clearly too small to hold fish large enough to be worth pursuing.

These minor excursions and investigations ate up time. It was just past noon when he finally came across a body of water that seemed large enough to support decent trout, but too small to attract much fishing pressure.

He slowed, got the Oldsmobile well off the road, and killed the engine. Consulting his map, he found no thin blue line to indicate the existence of the creek. This was promising, since it considerably reduced the possibility of the water receiving much attention. On the other hand, of course, there was no way of knowing how far up the mountain the stream went. But this uncertainty was one of the many things Willows liked about small-stream fishing. Encouraged, he refolded his map and tucked it back in the glove compartment, pushed open the door and stepped out of the car.

The creek was about twenty feet wide and perhaps three feet deep. A corrugated metal culvert funnelled it under the road. Willows estimated the flow rate at between eighty and a hundred gallons a minute. The bottom was rocky, with small pockets of sand. There was very little in the way of aquatic plant growth, probably as a result of the tumultuous scrubbing action of the annual spring floods.

Just as it entered the woods, the creek narrowed and turned sharply to the right, became a thin sliver of moving light that was quickly lost among the trees and thick undergrowth.

Willows liked what he saw. He traded his running shoes for the hip waders, put on his fishing vest, shrugged into the pack, and slung the leather rod case over his shoulder. A mile down the road, a huge articulated logging truck thundered towards him, the grillwork a bright gleaming speck at the head of a boiling roostertail of dust a thousand feet long and more than a hundred feet high.

Willows locked the car. He checked the boot. Then he began to make his way across the cleared strip towards the edge of the woods.

With each step he took, the waders rubbed together and made a faint squeaking noise. They were heavy and cumbersome, but he knew from past experience that without their protection the icy mountain water would numb his legs in minutes.

Except for the low muttering of the creek and the barely perceptible high-frequency whine of mosquitoes, the mountain was silent in the resinous midday heat.

Willows pushed upstream for the better part of an hour, moving slowly at first and then more quickly as he warmed up and his stride lengthened.

Pausing at a small pool to take a drink, he noticed the tracks of a cat in a flat muddy spot near the water's edge. He studied the tracks carefully, decided they had been left by a lynx and that they were fairly fresh, and followed them along the bank and then up a slight incline.

At the top it looked as if someone had shotgunned a feather pillow.

Crouching, Willows picked up the brown-and-grey barred breast feather of a Ruffed Grouse. He glanced around, looking for a fragment of bone or a rejected claw. But the bird had been young and tasty, and the lynx had done a good job of cleaning his plate. Only the explosion of feathers remained; insufficient evidence for all but the most rudimentary of autopsies.

Willows let go of the feather. It spiralled down to the surface of the water and was swept away by the current. He splashed water on his face and the back of his neck, and cheerfully resumed his journey.

Already, parts of the life he had left behind seemed impossibly distant, and it was easy for him to imagine that the city, with its busy population of thieves and murderers, had ceased to exist.

3

Mannie Katz was only thirty-two years old, but he rarely had any trouble passing for forty.

In repose his face was thin, sallow, and deeply lined. His sandy brown hair was limp and receding. There was a pouch of loose skin under his chin. His pores were enlarging. And in the mornings, standing bleary and defenceless in front of the bathroom mirror, he secretly admitted to himself that with each passing day he looked a little bit more like the picture on his driver's licence.

Mannie tried to minimize his physical shortcomings by spending a lot of money on clothes. So, usually, he looked like a very well dressed pear-shaped forty-year-old prematurely balding man.

But not tonight.

Tonight Mannie was wearing a generic brand shirt made of flimsy Taiwanese polyester; a tie that looked like a slice of neon pizza and was almost as wide as his chest; a shapeless bile-green suit with an inkstain under the pocket; and a pair of scuffed brown penny loafers so small they could have been bronzed. The shoes were a full two sizes too small and Mannie's feet were killing him. But he liked to think he had discipline. As he walked down the gentle slope of Davie Street, he forced himself to ignore the sharp little forkfuls of pain that accompanied each and every step he took.

Off to the left, the sun was about to fall into the Pacific Ocean. Above him, a trio of mosquito hawks dipped and wheeled erratically in the shadows of the surrounding highrises, their high-pitched cries of gluttony and pleasure bouncing and echoing off the concrete walls.

Mannie glanced at his watch. It was twenty minutes past nine. He was dead on schedule.

Limping noticeably, he walked past the restaurant. Three storeys high, it was built of massive blocks of rough-cut sandstone, and squatted magnificently in the middle of half a city block of prime real estate. At the front of the building, an immaculate expanse of lawn was neatly bisected by a driveway of interlocking pink brick that ran in an exact semi-circle through a miniature forest of carefully pruned shrubs and dwarf evergreens.

At the rear of the building, there was an alley and a gleaming black Econoline van. The van was parked up against a big Smithrite dumpster. The dumpster was full to the brim with expensive leftovers, but Mannie noticed that none of the dozens of flies buzzing around were wearing tuxedos. He leaned against the Smithrite, taking some of the weight off his feet. The shoes were murdering him, the level of pain just barely this side of tolerable. He told himself that next time he'd go the other way, buy a pair that were a couple of sizes too large and stuff them with old newspapers or maybe six pairs of socks. He shot the cuff of the bile-green suit. Twenty-five past nine. Now that the sun was down, the light was fading fast. Mannie took a quick, furtive look around, satisfying himself that the darkening alley was empty.

Sliding the knife out of its oiled leather sheath, he moved in on the van. His pace was unhurried and his back was erect. He looked as if he had every right to be there. Except for the knife, he looked perfectly harmless, even a little bit lost.

The knife was eight inches long. It had a weighted aluminium and composition slab handle and a deep, sharply curved blade. It had been designed to cut the lead strips that were used in the construction of stained-glass windows. The blade was high-quality carbon steel, forged in West Germany. Mannie had spent most of an afternoon applying the edge to an oilstone, and he had sharpened the blade so fastidiously that he was able to chop effortlessly through small bones with it.

Now he reversed the knife in his hand and used the handle to punch a ragged hole in the window on the driver's side of the van. When the hole was large enough to get his hand through, he reached inside, twisting his wrist at an awkward angle to get at the lock.

A door at the rear of the restaurant swung open. A rapidly widening beam of smoky yellow light splashed across the van. Mannie crouched, froze. He heard the clatter of pots and smelled but failed to identify béarnaise sauce. A bulky silhouette filled the doorway, an arm pointed accusingly at Mannie. Then a cigarette arced like a tracer through the air towards him, lost velocity and altitude, struck a shower of sparks on the asphalt.

The door slammed shut.

Mannie let out a little sigh. His heart started beating again. He unlocked the door and sheathed the knife and climbed into the van. Brushing away fragments of glass, he lay down on his back in the leg well with his head resting on the red shag carpet that covered the transmission hump. Taking a small magnetized flashlight from his pocket, he attached it to the steering column so the narrow beam shone up into the confusion of brightly coloured wires and cables that were hidden behind the dashboard.

Mannie was no electrician, but years of experience had given him plenty of confidence in his plodding methodology. Using a wire stripper, he peeled away half an inch or more of the protective plastic coating that covered the ignition wires, and then began to experiment with several short lengths of loose wire soldered at both ends to small alligator clips.

Twice he caused short circuits that resulted in brief fireworks displays, unpleasant smells and showers of sparks. Then the big V-8 engine turned over, and caught. The evening's first rush of adrenalin coursed through Mannie's veins. He pressed down hard on the gas pedal with the heel of his left hand. The engine howled and the van shuddered beneath him. He made sure the alligator clips were secure, and hauled himself up off the floor and into the driver's seat.

Looking anxiously around, he saw that the alley was still deserted. Nobody was paying any attention. It was just him and the flies. He rolled down the side windows and then kicked off his shoes, picked them up and twisted in his seat to throw them into the back of the van.

Surprise!

The floor, walls, and even the ceiling were carpeted in the same gaudy red plush that covered the transmission hump. The stuff was everywhere, even glued to the sides of the little bar fridge standing in a corner at the back.

Above the fridge there was a chrome rack holding two wine glasses. Diagonally opposite, suspended from the ceiling by a steel bracket, there was a small colour television. Most of the remaining space was taken by a low bed with a mirrored headboard and heart-shaped cushions, a bedspread of a silvery metallic material. A bordello on wheels. Mannie blinked, and turned away. He fiddled with the tape deck. A flood of syrupy music blared from hidden speakers. He turned down the volume, released the emergency brake, and put the van in gear.

At Jervis he stopped for a red light. He was only one short block from the intersection of Davie and Bute. Through the windscreen he could see the bank of open phone booths that were the main reason for the corner's popularity with the younger set.

He took a cigar packaged in an aluminium tube from the inner breast pocket of his suit. The cigar had cost three dollars, but Felix Newton was paying for it. Not that this was unreasonable, since Mannie had never been a smoker, and the only reason he had bought the cigar was because he liked the idea of a meaningless prop. Small deceptions had always been his idea of a good time. Probably that was one of the reasons he was so happy in his line of work.

He got the cigar out of the tube, bit off an end, stabbed at the lighter with his index finger. The traffic light changed. He pressed his stockinged foot down on the gas pedal, and the van powered smoothly through the intersection.

As he approached the corner, Mannie slowed to a crawl and then pulled in to the curb and stopped. There were half a dozen hookers loitering around the phone booths. Most of them were in their early teens. Mannie spotted the boy he was after. They made eye contact, and Mannie saw the boy stiffen. Mannie took the cigar out of his mouth and smiled broadly, ear-to-ear stuff, really stretching his face to the limit. The boy grinned puckishly back, raised a knowing eyebrow. He had a very nice complexion. His eyes were dark green, inviting. When he returned Mannie's smile, he displayed two rows of perfect teeth.

Mannie gave a little nod of his head and the boy started confidently towards the van, hands wedged deep in the pockets of his tight white linen trousers. Mannie let him get almost close enough to touch, then punched it. The boy took his hands out of his pockets. A look crossed his face as if he'd just bitten

20

into something with mould on it. Mannie watched him dwindle and then vanish into the tinted depths of his rearview mirror. He drove two blocks down Davie and took a left, parked in front of a brightly lit grocery store and got out of the van.

It was fully dark now. Although he could still hear the mosquito hawks hunting in the air high above him, he could no longer see them.

4

Willows pushed upstream for several more hours without encountering any fishable water. By late afternoon he was starting to tire, and to wonder if he was wasting his time. Then, without warning, he suddenly came upon a broad and sharply defined clearing, bright sunlight that made him squint and shield his eyes. He was standing at the tail of a pool perhaps sixty feet long and thirty feet wide at its widest point. To his right there was a meadow in the shape of an elongated oval, tall yellow summer grass and a profusion of wild daisies.

Willows slipped out of his pack and took a can of Black Label from one of the outer pockets. He stepped into the pool and put the beer in the cold water, twisting the can into the fine golden sand on the bottom so the current would not carry it away. Back on the bank, he sat down on a rock, kicked out of his waders and pulled off socks that were wet with perspiration. Wriggling his toes, he looked around.

On the far side of the pool there was a steep cliff, the top crowded with overhanging cedars. Here and there the afternoon sun streamed down through the widespread branches like celestial spotlights, sparkling on the water and giving it body and the appearance of depth. The face of the cliff dripped with run-off from above, and was blanketed with bright green moss, fat and glittery with moisture, and with a few precariously situated sword ferns.

Willows wrung out his socks and lay them down on the gravel bank to dry in the sun. He rolled up his twill trousers, took the few short steps to the water's edge, and tested the temperature with his toes. He waded slowly into the pool. With each cautious step he took, the water pulsed away from him in a little rolling wave that soon vanished in upon itself like a magician's trick. The flat, apparently motionless surface of the water seemed to act like a magnifying glass. Willows watched grains of sand eddy up around his feet, fall slowly back.

At the head of the pool, sixty feet away, there was the cliff, and opposite the cliff a boulder as large as a house but shaped exactly like the top half of an egg. In the narrow, constricted gap between the cliff and the rock, a short steep rapids churned and frothed noisily. Near the foot of the rapids a large cedar tree had lost its footing and toppled into the water, and its branches had been stripped clean of bark and foliage by the force of the churning current. Below the rapids, in the throat of the pool, the water was so deep that it was black.

If Willows couldn't quite taste his dinner, he could certainly smell it cooking.

He cupped his hands together and scooped water out of the creek, drank thirstily. When his thirst was quenched, he turned and waded slowly back out of the pool. Picking up his gear, he made his way through the bending grass and the tall white and yellow daisies, up to the high end of the meadow. In half an hour he had pitched his tent, dug a fire pit and gathered enough wood to last him through the evening. The chores completed, he retrieved the can of Black Label from the pool and unpacked his Waltonesque lunch of cheese, dark bread, and fresh fruit.

When the last of the crumbs were gone, he lay down in the grass with his head resting on his pack and the cold beer balanced on his chest. All around him the flowers swayed gently, cutting cookie shapes out of a flawless blue sky. He sipped at the last of the beer, and closed his eyes. The ground beneath him was spongy and soft, and he soon drifted into a deep sleep.

He slept for several hours, the alarm that finally awakened him a big pileated woodpecker banging away on a stump at the fringe of the meadow. He sat up and stretched, spreading his arms wide. The bird caught the movement and scuttled crab-like around to the far side of the stump. It continued to hammer away as he started a fire, using twigs for kindling and feeding the growing flames with chunks of vine maple salvaged from a nearby deadfall.

When the fire had steadied and was no longer throwing sparks, Willows took his coffee pot down to the tail end of the pool and filled it to the brim with cold, clear water.

It was early dusk, and at the head of the pool a trio of trout were feeding. One was working just below the rapids and the other two were some distance downstream. He watched the fish for a few minutes, and then carried the coffee pot back to the fire and stood it on his makeshift grill. The pot had an old-fashioned shape and was finished in a dark blue enamel speckled with a creamy white. Willows had owned the pot since his early teens. It was a much-treasured possession, one of those rare things that never seemed to wear out or outlast its usefulness, and that somehow became more valued as the years passed by.

Sitting on his heels, he eased the Hardy fly rod out of its leather case and fitted the two lengths of graphite together, carefully lining up the guides and then pushing the ferrules firmly home. His reel was also a Hardy, fitted with a very old double-tapered silk line and thirty yards of nylon cuttyhunk backing.

Willows seated the reel and screwed the locking ring tight. Then he fed the end of the fly line up through the guides and attached nine feet of three-pound-test nylon leader.

The leader was brand new, and hung in limp coils. Willows straightened it by pulling it several times through a piece of innertube pinched over upon itself.

When he was satisfied with his tackle, he put on his socks and waders and went back down to the tail end of the pool, where the bottom shelved quickly up and the swiftly flowing water had a glossy, taut look about it, as if compressing itself in its rush to escape the confines of the pool.

Standing knee-deep in the water, Willows saw four drowned wasps drift by in the space of only a few minutes. Now he knew what the fish were feeding on, or at least had been given a glimpse of the menu. He opened a hinged aluminium fly box, and selected a Western Bee on a number 8 hook. The fly was bulky and colourful, with a body of alternating bands of orange and black chenille, and blunt backswept wings of natural tan bucktail. He fastened the fly to the leader with a double turl knot. Finally, he fluffed the hackles so the fly would ride high on the water, denting but not penetrating the surface film; causing sparkles of light to radiate down to his quarry and stimulate a reflex response. Or so the theory went.

Crouching, keeping his profile low, Willows worked his way upstream.

The surrounding mountains had cut short the day, and the shadows of this early summer evening were already blurring the edges of things, making depth perception difficult. The footing in the shifting, deceptive light was tricky and uncertain. Willows moved cautiously into the pool until he was thigh deep, the pressure of the moving water firm and constant.

Behind him the bank sloped steeply upward, topped with a fringe of grass and a wild tangle of scrub brush. In this constricted space, Willows had no option but to try to reach the feeding trout with a roll cast. Stripping line from the reel, he pointed the tip of the rod at the water, and waggled it gently from side to side. Line slithered through the guides and was carried slowly downstream by the current. He gathered more line in loose coils in his left hand. Then, in a single fluid motion, he brought the rod sharply up until it was just past the vertical, twisted his wrist, and swept the rod forward and down. The line behind him lifted off the water in a rolling loop, the weight of it pulling the prepared coils from his left hand and through the guides.

Forty feet of line straightened in the air, hung motionless and then descended.

The Bee dropped lightly on the water within a reasonable distance of Willows' intentions. The cast was complete.

He retrieved a bit of slack.

The trout moved up through the blackness like a lightning bolt, striking viciously at the deceptive bundle of thread and feather and sharp steel.

Willows struck back, setting the barbless hook. The rod bowed and the line tightened, throwing a spray of mist that sparkled in the air like a fistful of powdered diamonds. The fish jumped. Willows dropped the rod's tip, trying to keep the line slack. The fish jumped again, twisting and turning like a length of animated neon. Then it sounded, dropping to the bottom of the pool to sulk and recover its strength. Willows hit the butt of the rod with the heel of his hand. The fish rose quickly, and shot towards him. He saw the black and orange of the fly in the corner of its mouth, and then it flared and raced back upstream, making a run for the downed cedar and tangle of pale yellow branches at the head of the pool. Willows struggled to gather

25

in the slack, but too late; the leader was snarled and he had lost contact with the fish.

Turning, he made his way carefully out of the water and back up on the beach. His line drifted downstream, bellied in the current. He could feel the living weight of the trout on the end of the line, now. But there was something else there too, something stiff and unyielding.

Intending to break off, Willows gradually increased the pressure on the line.

A human hand, the wide-spread fingers pale and bloated, rose slowly out of the water and then fell back with a splash.

Willows stood motionless, unwilling to believe his eyes. Surely what he had seen was nothing more ominous than a freak arrangement of branches? He raised the rod and the hand appeared again, puffy and splayed and very white. Then the leader snapped.

Willows slowly reeled in his line. The hand was on the far side of the pool, at the base of the cliff. To reach it he would have to make his way upstream past the rapids, find a place to cross and then circle back down.

He leaned his rod against the bank and started up the beach, gravel crunching under his boots. At the head of the pool he had to enter the woods to get around the huge, egg-shaped rock. It was tough-going through the thick brush, fallen trees, and waist-high salal.

He made his way back to the stream as quickly as he could, and by lucky accident came across a natural bridge; a pair of uprooted fir trees that straddled the creek. The trees were exactly parallel and no more than six inches apart. The gap between the trunks was filled with a long and intricate web of sand, pebbles, and small stones, each fragment and grain wedging its neighbours in place. Under different circumstances Willows would have paused to examine this strange jigsaw puzzle, a puzzle that seemed logically impossible to construct except all at once. But his mind, as he crossed the stream, was filled with recurring images of the dead hand rising from the water and falling back with a soundless splash.

Arms spread wide for balance, he crossed the creek and then climbed and slid down a rocky overgrown slope to the base of the falls.

The girl was naked.

She lay on her back, facing into the current. Her long blonde hair drifted languidly across her shoulders and small breasts, shifting endlessly in the confusion of currents. Her body was so badly swollen that it had a rubbery, pneumatic look.

On the third finger of her left hand a gold and diamond chip ring had almost been swallowed by the expanding flesh. There was a smudge of blue on the inside of her forearm. Leaning precariously out over the water, Willows saw that it was a tattoo.

The girl's left foot protruded a few inches above the surface of the water. Part of the fleshy pad at the base of her toes had been eaten away. Now Willows knew where the drowned wasps had come from.

Icy water slopped over the rim of a wader, trickled down his leg. Heart thumping, he retreated gingerly to safer ground. The rapids and sheer wall of the cliff conspired to keep him from getting close enough to the body to retrieve it. He was going to have to go for help, and that was something he couldn't do until the morning.

Stumbling repeatedly in the gathering darkness, he made his way back to the meadow. The fire had been reduced to a glowing heap of coals. The enamel coffee pot rumbled and hissed on the grate, belching miniature clouds of steam. Willows kicked the pot as hard as he could, sent it tumbling and clanking through the grass and sleeping flowers. He piled chunks of maple on the fire, poked at the embers with a stick. A handful of sparks blossomed and died. The tent, illuminated by the growing flames, was a pale blue triangle in the night. He fumbled in his pack for the mickey of Cutty Sark he'd wrapped in his spare pair of socks, unscrewed the metal cap and took a stiff drink.

High above him, the night sky was crammed and choked with stars. Somewhere in the darkness a saw-whet owl utttered its monotonous series of low, whistled notes. Behind him, mist rose from the creek and drifted silently across the meadow, and the stream muttered endlessly to itself, like a drunk slurring his words.

Willows imagined the trout holding position through the night, the black water flowing around their sleek shapes just as

27

it flowed over the corpse of the girl. He took another sip of the whiskey. He wondered how long the girl had been dead, and how she had died. It was nonsense, but he wished he hadn't left his revolver locked away in the boot of the Oldsmobile.

The saw-whet owl hooted again, despondently. There was a chill in the air. Willows picked up another piece of wood and threw it on the fire.

5

The boy caught the repeating bright orange flash of the turn signal in his peripheral vision, and turned just as the Econoline pulled up to the curb beside him.

The van had come from the opposite direction he'd expected, catching him by surprise. He made his face go blank. The driver smiled and waved, beckoning him over.

The boy hesitated. He didn't like vans. Street wisdom said stay away from them. Once you were in the back of one, nobody could see you. You were all alone. But business had been anything but brisk. He needed some cash, and he needed it badly. Taking his time, trying not to seem over-anxious, he sauntered across the sidewalk towards the gleaming vehicle.

The window on the passenger side was open. He rested his forearms on the sill and leaned inside. The first thing he saw was several gay magazines, some of them with the plastic wrappers still intact. Then, as his eyes adjusted to the dim interior, he took in the ridiculous red plush and the mirrored bed.

Mannie took the cigar out of his mouth. "Hi," he said, "my name's Opportunity and I'm in the mood for love." He patted the seat beside him. "Hop in, big fella. Let's talk contract."

The boy stared at Mannie, openly assessing him. He saw a man in his forties, maybe five foot nine inches tall, about twenty pounds overweight. Flabby, with watery blue eyes and a complexion like the inside of a bagel. Hair combed sideways across his scalp in a pathetic attempt to hide his bald spot. Big nose. Small mouth. And the hands nervously clasping the steering-wheel were the hands of a woman, soft and white.

The boy opened the door and got into the van.

Mannie saw a gap and pulled out into the traffic with a squeal of burnt rubber. The boy grabbed at the dashboard to steady himself. The van accelerated. He managed to slam the door shut.

Mannie held out his hand, fingers curled to form a tight little nest cradling a single bill folded into a square box so small it was impossible to tell the bill's denomination.

"It's a hundred," said Mannie.

Something about Mannie's voice made the boy believe him. He snatched at the little square of paper much as the trout had plucked the Western Bee from the roof of Jack Willows' mountain pool; instinctively and without conscious thought.

Mannie waved the empty aluminium tube. "Want a cigar, kid?"

The boy shook his head distractedly. His mind was wholly occupied with the money. The stiff, unyielding little box of paper was so tightly folded that he was afraid he might tear it. Lips pursed, he plucked at the crisp, accordioned edges.

At Broughton, Mannie spun the wheel sharply to the left without slowing down or signalling his turn. They cut diagonally across the intersection in front of two lanes of oncoming traffic. The van slewed, a horn blared. The lead car in the outside lane flicked its brights, washing them in light. Mannie squinted and swore and kept his foot on the gas. The rear end broke free, and there was a peculiar and very unpleasant impression of weightlessness. Then they were through the intersection and tearing up Broughton, parked cars tight on either side.

"Where you going?" the boy said. He was sitting bolt upright, radiating tension.

"Almost there," said Mannie. He glanced in the rearview mirror. Nobody was pursuing them. He tapped the brakes and turned right, down a narrow lane.

The boy frowned. He was about to say something when, abruptly, the paper box began to fall apart, blossoming in the dim light like a time-lapse flower. It was a hundred, all right. His first three-digit trick. He laid the bill across his thigh and tried to iron the wrinkles from Robert Borden's face with the palm of his hand.

The van bounced down the lane, headlights jabbing crazily through the night. Mannie shifted down into second gear. The nose dipped as they turned down a short, steeply pitched asphalt driveway and into the parking area beneath a stuccoed apartment block.

Light rippled on the short hood and near-vertical windscreen as they passed beneath row upon row of long fluorescent tubes. Mannie braked, and eased carefully into a slot bounded on one side by a concrete wall and on the other side by a dusty camper top on blocks. He put the van in neutral and yanked on the emergency brake. Turning towards the boy he suddenly wedged his hand between the seat and white trousers, grabbed a cheek and squeezed hard. The boy gasped and arced his back, struggling to get away. He cried out, his voice shrill.

"Hush!" warned Mannie.

The boy wriggled. "Just . . . tell me what you want me to do," he said.

Mannie gave him an enquiring look. "What do you like to do?"

"Whatever you want," the boy whispered.

Mannie had lied often enough to recognize the truth when he heard it. He realized that the Econoline had become an ersatz confessional; he a priest of the moment and the boy a penitent about to atone for a deficiency of character, flawed genes, an unfair share of bad luck. He looked at the boy, measuring the depths of his weaknesses and the vast breadths of his fears. Cigar ash spilled unnoticed down his chest, across the tie of many colours. He squeezed a little harder, kept up the pressure until there was no doubt in his mind that the boy knew who was in charge. Then he let go.

"Get in the back, kiddo."

The boy nodded. He was crouched in the narrow gap between the bucket seats when Mannie stabbed him in the small of his back. The force of the blow and his own momentum sent him tumbling across the foot of the bed. He opened his mouth to scream. Mannie fell on top of him, knocked the wind out of him. Blood gushed from his side. He felt Mannie's plump white fingers clawing at his scalp, pushing his face down into the silvery sheets. He tasted metal, his own sour bile.

Mannie tried to pull the knife out but it was stuck. He worked the blade up and down, savagely twisted it from side to side.

The boy wriggled and squirmed. He corkscrewed frantically across the bed. The knife came free. Blood geysered. Mannie drew back his arm so far that a seam in the bargain basement suit gave way with a strident ripping sound. He put the knife in again and hit bone, the force of impact jarring his arm all the way to the shoulder. The boy kicked out. The mirrored headboard exploded, showering them both in a storm of silvered glass.

Mannie stabbed and stabbed and stabbed again, splattering himself with tiny cutlets of flesh, digging like a frenzied archaeologist of the human soul. The air filled with a fine red mist that turned deep purple where it was touched by the fluorescents. Mannie felt himself tiring. He didn't let up.

Finally the boy made a raspy clotted sound deep in his throat, and went limp.

Exhausted, Mannie fell back against a wall of red shag. His breathing was fast and shallow and ragged. He was hyperventilating. He felt dizzy and disoriented, as if he'd just been whacked on the gyroscope. Letting go of the knife, he closed his eyes.

When his heart had slowed to the point where he could distinguish individual beats, he wiped gore from the crystal of his watch and saw that a little over twenty minutes had passed since he'd bagged the van.

Wearily, he made his way back to the driver's seat. There was a full box of Kleenex on the shelf under the glove compartment. The box was decorated with a variety of cartoon animals that had found a use for the product. Mannie used most of the box to scrub the blood from his hands and face. When he was finished, he pulled off his suit jacket. There was blood all down the front of his shirt, so he took that off too. Then he put the van in reverse and backed out of the parking slot.

His hands, as he drove, were slippery on the wheel. The blood was gone, but now he was sweating. Directly above him, the rows of fluorescents made a faint crackling sound, like distant laughter.

Mannie listened for a moment, and then joined in. Tears streamed down his cheeks. He laughed so loudly that he frightened himself.

And when he tried to stop laughing, he found he couldn't.

6

Eddy Orwell arrived at the door of Claire Parker's apartment at eight-thirty sharp. Parker lived on the third floor of an old converted Victorian house. Orwell buzzed himself in and took the carpeted steps two and three at a time, the snubbie in its shoulder holster bouncing against his chest.

At the door, he paused to take his pulse. It had accelerated from its usual 48 beats per minute to more than 120 bpm, but Orwell was confident that the swift ascent had little or nothing to do with the increased rate. He was in great shape. It was his emotional state of mind that had sent the blood thundering through his veins. He straightened his dark blue tie, combed his brush-cut with his fingers, and knocked on Parker's door with a fist the size of a large coconut.

Parker answered the door wearing six-inch spikes and a pleated black skirt, a white blouse with a high collar. Orwell felt the wind go out of him. In the heels, she was exactly one inch taller than he was, which didn't do anything at all for his ego. Also, in those clothes, she looked more like a cop than a hot date. But he smiled up at her anyway, because he thought she looked terrific despite everything. He had an almost overpowering urge to take her in his arms, bury his nose in her glossy black hair, nibble at the lobe of a perfect ear, and see what happened next.

Parker saw the look in his eyes. She'd seen that look before. She knew exactly what it meant, and she knew exactly how to deal with it.

"I worked all through lunch, Eddy, and I didn't get home until seven. I'm starving, and the thought of showing up late and finding that we lost our reservation does not make me feel all soft and warm inside."

"No problem," said Orwell. "First things first, right?"

"What's that supposed to mean?"

Orwell shrugged. He grinned his pirate's grin, conscious that his large, square teeth were very white against his midsummer tan. He lounged against the wallpaper while Parker locked up. This was their third date in less than two weeks. Orwell hadn't been offered a key, and he wasn't quite dumb enough to ask for one.

The restaurant Orwell had chosen was located on Stanley Park's Ferguson Point. When he'd told Parker where they were going, he thought he'd seen a flash of irritation in her chocolate-brown eyes. But he wasn't sure, the moment had come and gone and she hadn't said anything. So he'd let it go.

Stanley Park is a thousand acres of mostly untended vegetation. It's shaped like an elephant's head, is situated at the west end of the city, and is surrounded on three sides by the Pacific Ocean.

The restaurant was renowned for its fabulous view of the outer harbour, and Orwell had reserved a window table. The restaurant was, by his standards, very expensive. But he had a little surprise tucked up his sleeve, and he was willing to pay almost any price to ensure that this would be an evening the two of them would remember with warmth and affection for the rest of their lives.

Orwell didn't argue with Parker when she suggested they take her Volkswagen, and leave his rusted Ford Fairlane at the curb. He was having problems with the automatic choke, and the car kept dying on him. He hadn't fixed the Fairlane because he was thinking about buying a new car.

Parker drove quickly and well. They arrived at the Point with ten minutes to spare, and parked on the road several hundred feet beyond the restaurant. Orwell noticed that Parker didn't bother to lock her door when she got out of the car. He almost mentioned the skyrocketing crime rate, but managed to restrain himself. Nothing was going to spoil the evening. He simply wouldn't allow it to happen.

Probably because the restaurant was owned by the Parks Board, it had no bar. The Maître d' greeted them warmly, as if they were old friends. Without delay, he led them through an archway of filigreed plaster and into the arboretum – a huge dome shaped like an upturned wine glass with the stem knocked off.

The air was warm and humid, heavy with moisture. Each of

the thirty or more tables was surrounded by a miniature jungle of exotic tropical plants. The light level was very low. Somewhere off to Orwell's left a flock of birds muttered peevishly, their voices low and insistent, vaguely troubled. Orwell knew that there really weren't any birds. Three days earlier, when he'd cased the restaurant, he'd learned that the sound of their voices came from an endless tape.

In single file, Parker and Orwell followed the Maître d' along a narrow winding path of crushed white stone. All around them, candles flickered uncertainly; faint yellow sparks of warmth that only seemed to emphasize the depth of the surrounding gloom. It was a weird place. Orwell was just beginning to wonder if he'd rather be somewhere else when they arrived at their table, and all his worries and uncertainties fled in a moment.

Out on the purpling water a dozen freighters rode hull-down on the ebb tide; a handful of sailboats tacked sluggishly into a fitful wind; and a deepsea tug hauled a huge pyramid of sawdust towards the curving rim of the horizon, into the heart of a fat orange sun.

"Beautiful view," said Orwell appreciatively.

"Thank you," said the Maître d'.

"If you like postcard art," said Parker.

Orwell frowned. The Maître d' busied himself arranging the menus and wine list on the cramped little table. He drew back a wicker-chair for Parker, and tried to look down her neckline when she sat down. Almost as an afterthought, he wondered if they might be interested in an apéritif.

"Champagne," said Orwell decisively.

"Domestic, or imported, Sir?"

"French."

"We have Charles Heidsieck, Mumm's . . ."

Orwell cut him off with a wave of his hand. "Just bring us whatever's most expensive."

"Of course."

"And make sure it's real cold. Put lots of ice in the bucket."

"Yes, certainly."

Parker leaned towards Orwell, resting her elbows on the table. She still wasn't sure why she was going out with Orwell. To help her forget about her brief fling with Jack Willows, probably. She'd thought Orwell safe enough, because she wasn't really attracted to him and because she'd heard he was serious about a woman named Judith Lundstrom. Maybe that's what the champagne was all about. Orwell was planning to drop her, let her down easy. Or was that just wishful thinking? She smiled at him and said, "What's going on, Eddy?"

"Nothing," said Orwell, maybe a little too loudly. "So tell me, how was work?"

"Let's not talk shop, okay?"

"Fine, fine. Whatever you say." Orwell held up his hands in a gesture of mock submission, displaying palms that were padded and swollen with thick callouses built up during the endless hours he'd spent pumping iron at Gold's gym.

"And please don't try to change the subject, either. Why the champagne?"

"No reason, really. Just a whim."

Parker stared suspiciously at him, but didn't say anything. Silence was often an interrogator's most effective tool.

Orwell smiled nervously. He fiddled with his silverware, wiped his sweating hands on a thick white linen napkin that had too much starch in it. He adjusted the knot of his tie. He frowned.

Parker leaned back in her chair. High above her, the wavering lights of dozens of candles were reflected in the convex glass of the ceiling, like so many distant stars. She leaned back a little more, so that she could take in the entire tableau, and tried to work out which spark of light came from their particular table. A palm frond tickled her ear. She reached behind her and briskly detached it from the main stem.

Orwell pretended not to have noticed. Lowering his eyes, he solemnly studied the prices on the menu.

A white-coated waiter arrived with the champagne, a silver ice-bucket and a pair of tulip-shaped glasses. He put the glasses and the bucket down with a restrained flourish, stripped the foil from the neck of the bottle and deftly removed the wire cage enclosing the bulbous cork. Orwell watched him carefully, memorizing every move he made. The cork pulled free with a festive pop. The mouth of the bottle smoked like a gun. The waiter placed the cork on the table in front of Orwell, and filled his glass just a bit too full. Orwell tasted the champagne. It was so cold it made his teeth ache. He swallowed, and nodded his approval. A flurry of golden bubbles jostled upwards and commited mass suicide in a futile attempt to make him sneeze.

The waiter indicated Orwell's menu. "Are you ready to order, Sir?"

"No, not quite."

"I've never eaten here before," said Parker. "Is there anything you recommend?"

The waiter hesitated, visibly pondering, his eyes on her face. "The pheasant's very good this evening," he said at last.

"Then I'll have the pheasant," said Parker, smiling.

The waiter cocked his head at Orwell, and the gold chains around his neck glinted in the light.

"Pheasant for two," said Orwell. He picked up the wine list.

"We've found the Pouilly-Fuisse goes very well," the waiter offered.

Orwell, studying the wine list, didn't notice the waiter give Parker a conspiratorial wink. He found the wine right at the bottom of the list, priced at $42.50. He bit his lip, thinking hard.

"Pouilly-Fuissé it is," said Parker.

Orwell picked up the broken palm frond. He held it over the candle flame. The frond twisted and writhed fitfully, as if trying to escape. Orwell watched it shrink, turn black from the heat. When it began to smoke he let it drop negligently to the floor.

"Is something wrong?" said Parker.

"No, of course not."

"Nothing's bothering you?"

"I'm fine. Perfect."

Parker drained her glass and reached for the bottle.

"Let me get it," said Orwell.

Parker ignored him. She gripped the heavy bottle with both hands and pulled it from the ice bucket. Water dripped on the tablecloth. She filled her glass and offered the bottle to Orwell, then plopped it back in the bucket. Water spilled over the lip of the bucket and splashed on the carpet. He watched her pick up her glass, carry the glass carefully to her lips. He noted with a sense of wonder the movement of her slim and graceful throat as she swallowed.

For the hundredth time, he told himself she was the most

beautiful woman he had ever seen, and that he could not possibly live without her.

Parker caught him looking. He blushed like a kid on his first date, the suffusion of blood turning his skin a dull red, the colour of porch paint.

By the time they'd finished their pheasant, the sun had set and the horizon was dark. Nothing remained of the bird but the backbone and a few jutting ribs, a congealing pool of blood and gravy. The champagne was long gone and they were on their second bottle of wine. Parker's drinking had slowed down, but Orwell had picked up the slack. He was feeling very relaxed. A thick film of grease lay on his glass. He held the glass up against the unsteady light of the candle, turning it this way and that, admiring the clarity of his fingerprints. Wine trickled down his chin. He dabbed at himself with a napkin. A sliver of meat caught his attention. He winkled it free with his thumbnail, chewed, drank some more wine.

Parker smiled across the table at him. "You still hungry, Eddy?"

Orwell shook his head. "No, not really." Just nervous as hell, that's all.

"Want some dessert?"

"I'm too full. How about you?"

"Coffee would be nice."

"If we can find our waiter," said Orwell. "I think he went off shift about an hour ago. Next time we come here, let's remember to pack a flare gun." He picked up the bottle and tipped the last inch of wine into Parker's glass.

"Are you trying to get me drunk?"

"I thought it was the other way around," said Orwell. The look on Parker's face encouraged him to add hastily: "Hey, just kidding." He raised his glass, and saw that it was empty, and put it back down on the table in front of him with a heavy thud.

Parker studied her watch. "It's been a nice evening, Eddy. But I've had a long day, and tomorrow isn't going to be any easier."

"I thought you had tomorrow off," said Orwell.

"So did I."

"Listen, there's something I've got to tell you." Both Parker and Orwell had spoken at exactly the same moment, their voices in perfect synchronization, as if they'd been rehearsing for months. They stared warily at each other. Parker recovered first.

"Go ahead, Eddy."

"Ladies first."

"Don't be ridiculous."

Orwell had been waiting all through the meal for the right moment to make his move. But the right moment had never seemed to come. And now, suddenly, it had been forced upon him. Covertly, he slipped his hands inside the pocket of his suit jacket. The small sterling silver box felt smooth and cold. He flipped open the lid and ran the ball of his thumb over the faceted surface of the diamond. Half a carat. Eighteen hundred and fifty bucks. What with his health club dues and a few other odds and ends, he'd pushed his Amex card right to the limit.

Parker asked him if something was wrong, and he had said no. But that was a lie. Something was terribly wrong. He'd planned to ask her to marry him as soon as the champagne was poured, but the fucking waiter had kept hanging around. Next thing he knew the food was already on the table and his mouth was too full to talk. Why he'd eaten so much, he couldn't say, especially since he'd hardly tasted a thing. And now, suddenly, the meal was over. They were about to leave and he had blown it, had failed to summon up the courage to ask for the hand of his own true love.

Frustrated, he snapped shut the hinged lid of the little box on the delicate web of flesh between his thumb and first finger, and gave a little yelp of surprise and pain.

"What's wrong?" said Parker.

The waiter hurried up, looking concerned. Orwell glared at both of them, and flung his credit card down on the table like a gauntlet.

Outside, the air was fresh and sweet after the warm, humid, cloying atmosphere of the restaurant. There was a cool breeze coming in from the ocean, across the mouth of the harbour, and they could hear the leaves rustling in the trees behind them, a gentle whispering above the wail of a distant siren. High above them, the night sky was crowded with real stars – the genuine article, and not stars of wax. Orwell filled his lungs, exhaled slowly. He and Parker walked slowly across an open expanse of lawn towards her car.

"Lots of ships out there tonight," said Orwell, taking in the expanse of restless black water and the scattered ovals of light with a negligent wave of his hand.

"Freighters," said Parker.

After a moment Orwell said, "Let's count them."

"Why?"

"I don't know. Just for the hell of it." Orwell was experiencing sudden bouts of double vision, but he was nobody's fool. Half a bottle of champagne and the better part of two bottles of white wine had not entirely eliminated his ability to think like a fox.

Cunningly, he squeezed shut his left eye. "One," he said. "Two . . . three . . ."

With each step Orwell took across the grass, his perspective seemed to shift and jump, the horizon tilted, and the relative positions of the ships was altered radically. Also, there was a tugboat off to his right somewhere, and the monotonous throbbing of the powerful diesel engines was giving him a killer headache.

They were almost at her car when Parker said, "You finish counting yet?"

"Just about," said Orwell. Cannily, he said, "How about you, what'd you get?"

"Eleven," said Parker.

Orwell dived headlong for the opening. "Me too," he said. "On the nose."

They were very close to the car now, crossing the parking lot side by side. Parker fumbled in her bag for her keys, dropped them jangling to the asphalt. Orwell knelt and scooped them up, lost his balance and had to brace himself. He gave her the keys. To his left, a sloppily parked Corvette was crowding the Volkswagen. Orwell had trouble opening the car's door wide enough to get in.

Parker turned the key in the ignition. The black skirt had ridden high up on her thighs. She appeared to be unaware of how much leg she was showing, and Orwell decided not to notice. He wasn't going to pop the question in the car. Instead, he was going to suggest that they go back to his apartment for a nightcap. Once there, he'd turn down the lights, pour a couple of stiff brandies, mix in some mood music and pick his spot.

Parker revved the engine, put the Volks in reverse and gently let out the clutch. The car started to creep backwards. She spun the wheel with both hands, arcing the nose away from the Corvette.

Orwell couldn't stop himself. He leaned across the seat and put his hand on her thigh, nuzzled her neck and tried to stick his tongue in her ear.

"Cut it out, Eddy."

Parker pushed him away. There was the loud crunch of metal impacting on metal, the snap-crackle-pop of safety glass shattering. The Volkswagen lurched to an abrupt stop, rocked on its springs, and was still.

"Nice going," said Parker. "Really terrific."

"Hey," said Orwell, "it wasn't my fault. *I* wasn't driving."

Parker shifted from reverse to first gear, gave the Volkswagen enough gas to disengage. More glass tinkled on the pavement. She turned off the engine and reached across Orwell to flip open the glove compartment. There was a flashlight in there somewhere. It was about the size of her little finger, and the battery was weak, but the thing worked. She got out of the car to assess the damage.

The vehicle she'd hit was parked on her side of the Volkswagen. It was a jet black Econoline van, and the front bumper looked as if someone had hit it with a bowling ball. Parker tried the door. It wasn't locked. She opened the door and sat down on the edge of the bucket seat, half in and half out of the van, her legs dangling. She aimed the yellow beam of the flashlight at the steering column, looking for the registration papers. Incidental light gleamed on dark plastic, chrome trim. A row of glass disks on the dashboard shone like mirrors.

The beam of the flashlight moved along. And stopped.

Parker's mind registered the tangle of stripped wires and the alligator clips dangling beneath the steering-wheel. She saw a rumpled suitcoat, and among the folds of dark green cloth a shining length of metal that looked like the barrel of a gun, but on closer inspection proved to be nothing more sinister than an empty aluminium cigar tube.

The weakening beam moved over and down, across a blizzard of Kleenex, the tissue stained dark red.

There was a noise behind her. She turned and saw Orwell getting out of the Volks.

"Stay right there, Eddy. Don't move an inch."

"Why," said Orwell. "What's the problem?"

Crouching, Parker directed the faltering cone of light into the back of the van. The glossy pages of a pornographic magazine splashed light back at her. The stiff, clawed fingers of a blood-streaked hand seemed to scuttle sideways as the shadow of the hand moved beneath the moving beam of light. She saw the slashed bed, tufts of foam rubber mattress. A smooth white face. Lacquered eyes. A mouth that hung wide open and might still have been screaming. A shirt of red and black, with more holes in it than a cribbage board.

In shock, Parker started to count the wounds.

A black car sped past, tape-deck blaring, tyres whining on the asphalt. The sudden intrusion startled Parker, got her thinking again. She switched off the flashlight and yanked her Smith & Wesson out of her purse.

Backing out of the van, taking care not to touch anything, she called out, "Okay Eddy, let's go."

"What?" said Orwell. His voice was smudged. He was sobering rapidly, but he was still a long way from legal. Parker grabbed him by the arm and led him away from the scene of the crime, towards the bright lights of the restaurant. Parker was with the city of Vancouver's serious crimes squad. Solving homicides was part of her job. As she hustled a confused Eddy Orwell back across the lawn, she was thinking that probably the first person she should phone was her partner, Jack Willows.

Then she remembered that Willows had gone fishing, and that he wasn't due back in the city for another two days . . .

7

Mannie adjusted the temperature of the water until it was so hot it hurt. He stepped under the spray and slid shut the pebbled glass door. Water drummed on his skull and poured down his face, into his eyes. His shoulders reddened. He tasted salt – a legacy of his recent ocean voyage.

There was a narrow green belt between the beach and the parking lot where he had dumped the van. Once he had reached this cover, Mannie stripped down to his bathing suit. He rolled his sticky bundle of cheap clothes into a ball and flung the ball high into the fork of a tree. Then he strolled down to the sea wall, across the sand, and into the ocean.

When he was about fifty feet out, he paused to tread water and orient himself. The sky was crowded with stars. Tinker Bell had been putting in overtime. Whispered conversations and soft laughter floated across the waves. Mannie smelled beach smoke, and hot dogs. He started swimming again, taking a course that would bring him to shore about two hundred yards away from the point where he had entered the water.

It took him a quarter of an hour to walk the mile of winding seawall to English Bay. The sight of a man in a bathing suit was not unusual; no one paid any attention to him.

His towel, cords, leather sandals and Lacoste polo shirt lay exactly as he had left them, in a tidy pile at the end of a log. His wallet and car keys were also as he'd left them, buried under six inches of sand. He picked everything up, went into the big concrete changing room and dressed. His bathing suit was still damp. He squeezed a few drops of water out of the material, rolled the suit up in the towel, and went back outside.

Hum of soft rubber wheels on asphalt. Blur of music. Mannie looked up as a black girl wearing a red and white diagonal striped bathing suit shot by on roller-skates. A portable radio was strapped to her narrow waist. Her hair was twisted into two stiff braids that stuck out over her head like antennae. She looked like a mobile barber's pole. Mannie watched her undulate into the darkness. Murder always made him horny, why was that? He started up the concrete steps to street level, the slap of his sandals seeming to applaud his every step.

The water was cooling. Mannie stooped to adjust the mix of hot and cold. He massaged a pale green worm of shampoo into his scalp, rinsed, shampooed, and rinsed again. Turning to face the spray, he used a nail-brush to get rid of the black crescents of dried blood beneath his fingernails.

When he was satisfied that he'd washed the last of the evidence down the drain, Mannie turned off the shower. He pushed back the pebbled glass door, slipped on the Chinese silk robe with the gold dragons crawling all over it. He wiped his face with a towel and then blow-dried his sparse hair. When his hair was dry he used the stream of hot air to clear a patch of condensation from the mirror. No sign of guilt in those pale blue eyes. The smile as friendly and spontaneous as it had ever been. Satisfied with his appearance, he went into the kitchen and pulled a Molson's Light out of the fridge.

He drank the beer straight from the can, standing in front of the open refrigerator with his feet spread for balance and his head tilted well back.

Hilda must have heard him, or noticed the kitchen light come on. She meowed as she came in from the back yard. Mannie took another sip of his beer and then went over to the sink and cracked open a tin of ersatz tuna. He forked the stuff into the cat's bowl and stood back. Hilda purred as she ate; a trick of the vocal cords Mannie very much admired. He drank his beer and watched his cat eat her dinner. It was ridiculous, but the smell of the viscous pink food had triggered his appetite. He was salivating.

There was a dark brown loaf of Winnipeg Rye on the counter, fresh that morning. In the fridge Mannie found a wedge of cheddar, mayonnaise, iceburg lettuce, a brick of unsalted butter, sweet pickles drifting in a jar of cloudy liquid. Working fast, Mannie made himself a double-decker four inches thick. He opened his mouth wide and was about to take his first bite when the telephone rang.

He knew who it was. He'd been expecting and dreading the call. Reflexively, he moved to pick up the telephone.

But then, because he liked to think he was his own man, he hesitated; took a big bite out of the sandwich, chewed deliberately, rinsed out his mouth with the last of the beer and got a second can out of the fridge.

Finally, on the ninth ring, he picked the instrument up and said: "Talk to me."

"You're up kind of late tonight, big fella. Got something to celebrate?"

The voice was deep and abrasive, a slow, southern Californian drawl. Mannie could almost see the waves as they came crashing in on the beach, hear the rocks grinding together in the surf. He pressed the receiver tightly to his ear, and said nothing. He and Felix Newton had a very concise relationship: when Felix spoke, everybody listened. No exceptions, even for wild and crazy guys like Mannie. Either you learned to catch the short side of the monologue, or you kind of faded from view without anybody noticing.

"You hear me?" said Felix.

"It's the weekend, that's all. Party time."

"Somebody there with you?"

"Just Hilda."

"What happens, you buy her a mouse and the three of you dance until dawn?"

"Hey," said Mannie. "That's a good one."

"Or maybe the two of you crack open a six-pack and watch a little TV."

"Not since Barney Miller retired."

"You telling me you missed tonight's news?"

"What news is that?"

"Somebody chopped up a kid and dropped his body in the park."

"What park is that?"

"Stanley Park."

"A nice park," said Mannie. "If I was a body, it's where I'd like to get dumped."

There was a long silence. Finally Felix said, "I'll try to remember that, Mannie."

"Don't go out of your way, Felix."

Felix Newton laughed, making a sound deep in his throat like coal rumbling down a long, dirty black chute. "You're a fun guy, Mannie. We ought to see a little more of each other, don't you think?"

"Sounds good."

"Maybe you could give me a few hours of your time later this week?"

"Yeah, sure."

"Squeeze me into your busy schedule, somehow?"

"You in town?"

"We could have brunch, okay?"

"Fine."

"I'll send Junior around in his new car, would you like that?"

"If it isn't too much trouble."

"Dress for white wine, you know what I mean?"

"What?" said Mannie, frowning.

Felix Newton hung up.

Some men ate raw oysters, others consumed powdered elk horns, or sought renewed vigour in the flesh of children. But the only aphrodisiac that had ever worked for Mannie was danger. Every time he yanked open a door, he hoped it was the one with the tiger crouched behind it. Or so he told himself. But Felix Newton gave him the creeps. The long, ominous, thoughtful silence that had followed his remark about being dumped in the park had not been a pleasant thing to listen to. And there was a persistent rumour that the last guy who'd annoyed Felix had been ground up like hamburger and fed to Felix's guppies.

Mannie finished his second beer, and most of a third. He got his Visa card out of his wallet and dialled a downtown number. A woman with a fake French accent answered on the first ring. Mannie gave her his card number and expiry date. As he spoke he could hear the quiet chattering of a computer keyboard in the background. The woman asked him if he was still living at the same address. He said, Why not, he got along okay with the neighbours and finally had the crabgrass on the run. Faint murmurs of repressed amusement. Did he have anything particular in mind?

You bet.

Tonight, he wanted a Japanese woman. Preferably a lady in her late twenties. Someone who'd just arrived in the country and didn't speak a single word of English. She had to be submissive, naturally, but also passionate and eager to learn Western ways. Was there a problem?

There was no problem. Mannie's personal file had blossomed on the amber screen of the computer's monitor seconds after he had finished reading out the number of his credit card. He had a reputation for tipping generously. Even more important, he was a pussycat in the sack, unimaginative and easily pleased.

All the girls liked him.

8

The stripped-down interior of the Sikorsky S-76's cargo hold
was all bare, unpainted metal. The incurving walls and low
ceiling were metal. The thin, dully gleaming skin of the floor
was metal. Even the perforated bucket seat Jack Willows sat
on was metal. He braced himself against a protruding metal rib
as the helicopter dipped and the flank of the mountain slid in
on them and then fell away, a dizzying blur of green.

Willows was sitting behind and slightly to the left of the pilot,
his back against a riveted bulkhead. Rossiter had the co-pilot's
seat. The second mountie, a man named Dickie, sat directly
opposite Willows. They were so close their knees almost
touched.

Nobody said anything. There was too much noise from the
pair of Allison turboshafts, the main and tail rotors, and the
junkyard bouncing around in the rear of the cargo hold: odd-
shaped chunks of iron, outsized tools with no obvious function.
A stack of threaded steel bolts half an inch thick and five feet
long, an electric motor salvaged from a dead washing machine.
What looked like part of a child's backyard swing set. A red
painted five-gallon can of gasoline and the big Husqvarna
chain-saw Dickie had hauled out of the boot of the RCMP
cruiser.

The tin-can acoustics doubled the racket: the echo was at
least as bad as the original noise. And, anyway, all the
questions had been asked down on the logging road, during the
long wait for the helicopter: Dickie standing a shade too close
to Willows, a hunter's look in his small dark eyes; Rossiter
silent, hardly there at all, maybe a little bit upset by Dickie's
enthusiasm for the cross-examination, but not speaking up.
There was something between the two men, but Willows had
no idea what it was.

The pilot turned, gestured towards Willows, and then
pointed down. Willows twisted in his seat as much as his seat-

belt would allow. Through the dirty plexiglass of the downward vision window he saw a thin trickle of silver, the small blue rectangle of his tent. Off to one side the distorted shadow of the Sikorsky took a bite out of the edge of the meadow where Willows had seen the pileated woodpecker. He noted that even when the machine was hovering, it seemed full of motion.

The whine of the engines increased in pitch. They swung around the meadow in a wide oval, and then Willows felt his stomach lurch as they lost altitude and the abstract of greens and blues below him turned into a detailed and very realistic landscape of rocks, grass, the white froth of the waterfall.

There was no need for him to point out the girl's body. From thirty feet up, it was impossible not to see.

The pilot moved his machine laterally, inch by inch. With a main rotor diameter of forty-four feet, there wasn't a lot of room to spare. Willows watched the sword ferns on the face of the cliff whip back and forth in the turbulence, as if seeking desperately to escape the wind and noise.

The nose dipped. There was a small thump and then a much larger one as they touched down.

The wash from the blades made Willows' tent puff up like a balloon. A perfect circle of daisies lay down as if in homage. The ashes of the dead campfire sprang up into the air and vanished. Willows blinked as Dickie slid open the starboard side door and the afternoon sun hit him full in the face. He smelled exhaust fumes, hot engine oil. The shrill whining in his ears slowly faded. Looking around, he had no sense at all of déjà vu.

The pilot switched off. Rossiter unbuckled his safety-belt, jumped out of the helicopter and started across the meadow towards the creek. Dickie stuck a spark plug wrench in the back pocket of his jeans and picked up the can of gasoline and the Husqvarna. He was maybe an inch under six foot, but his weight made him seem shorter. He had a regulation haircut, close-set eyes, a big nose with wide, flaring nostrils. His hair was blond but his bristly, aggressive moustache had a reddish tinge. He wasn't very light on his feet, but he looked strong. Crouched in the doorway, he turned to Willows and said: "You get the stretcher." Then he went out the hatch in a paratrooper's stance, as if they were still a couple of thousand feet up.

Willows half-expected him to yell Geronimo. The pilot said it instead, but softly. Grinning, Willows scooped up the portable stretcher and followed Dickie out of the helicopter.

Rossiter was standing on the low, brush-choked bank that had given Willows so much trouble with his back-cast. He didn't pay any attention when Willows and Dickie walked up. Staring out over the water, he snapped a small twig from a branch and busied himself stripping away the bark.

Willows looked down at the gravel beach. There were many small puddles where, overnight, his footsteps had filled to the brim with seepage. He noticed that the scale of things seemed to have changed. The bright light of day, the presence of the other men, and the looming bulk of the Sikorsky made the meadow and stream appear much smaller than they had before.

He watched Dickie unscrew the spark plug from the Husqvarna, examine the gap with a critical eye, run a thumbnail across the firing tip. Satisfied, Dickie screwed the plug back into place, tightened it with a quick twist of the wrench. He checked the oil level and wiped his hands on his jeans. Willows could see he was the type who liked to tinker, didn't mind getting a little grease under his nails. It should have made Dickie more likeable, but somehow it didn't.

Dickie adjusted the choke and gave the starter cord a yank. The engine fired immediately. He gave it some gas and switched it off.

"Somebody's got to go upstream and get over to the other side and cut the body loose," Dickie said, still hunched over the saw.

"You going to volunteer?" said Rossiter.

"Yeah, sure."

"Because I'll do it, if you don't want to."

"No," said Dickie, "it's okay. I don't mind at all."

Rossiter smiled. "In fact you're kind of looking forward to it, aren't you?"

"What the fuck is that supposed to mean?" Dickie stood up, the wrench still in his hand. Rossiter looked at the wrench. Dickie stuck the wrench in his back pocket and picked up the chain-saw. "How far am I going to have to go before I can get across?" he said to Willows.

Willows indicated the egg-shaped boulder. "Just the other side of that rock."

Dickie nodded. He turned his back on Willows and Rossiter and trudged along the bank, moving purposefully through the grass and scrub.

Rossiter chewed on his twig. "You're probably wondering why we get along so well," he said.

Willows shrugged noncommittally.

"Last week, Tuesday night, we busted a local kid. He'd broken into the hardware store, set off a silent alarm. We chased him for about three blocks, on foot. He ran down a lane, started to climb over a fence. We yelled at him to stop, but he kept going. Just as he was going over the top, Dickie shot him in the hip."

Rossiter examined the frayed end of the twig, spat out a fragment of pulp.

"See, the point is we'd had a good look at him and we both knew who he was. All we had to do was wait a while and then drive over to his parents' house and pick him up."

"But Dickie couldn't wait?"

"He's the kind of guy who's always in a hurry, if you know what I mean." Rossiter stared venomously after Dickie's retreating back. "I'm going to wade out and catch the body when it comes downstream. You want to give me a hand?"

"You make it sound so easy."

"Well then, let's do it as if it was."

"I'll be back in a few minutes," said Willows. "Call me if you need help."

He walked back past the helicopter and struck his tent, searched for and found the battered coffee pot. When he had all his gear together, he stowed it away in the Sikorsky. The pilot sat in the shade of his machine, his back against a strut. There were two empty coke cans between his sprawled legs, a third can in his lap. When a fly landed on the lip of the can he was drinking from, he made no effort to shoo it away.

Willows unlaced his boots and put on his waders. He walked back to the stream and found Rossiter squatting at the edge of the water in his jockey shorts.

Dickie had managed to get into position on the far side of the creek, at the foot of the waterfall. Willows watched him

51

lower the chain-saw to the ground, put a foot on the carrying handle, bend over the machine and suddenly straighten. There was a puff of thick blue smoke. A split second later Willows heard the harsh crackle of the engine. Dickie picked up the chain-saw. He leaned cautiously out over the water, his arms fully extended. Bright sunlight bounced off the wide blade.

Willows waded into the river. Rossiter followed him, swearing at the first shock of the icy water.

Fifty feet upstream, Dickie thrust the tip of the saw into the water and let out the clutch. A frothy white column of river jetted back at him, hit him square in the chest and face. He jerked back and then leant forward again, putting his weight into the work.

Sawdust began to drift past Willows, and small jagged pieces of yellow, freshly cut wood. Dickie leant a little harder into the saw. Willows saw him stagger, topple over, and then vanish beneath the boiling surface of the water at the foot of the rapids.

"Jesus Christ!" shouted Rossiter.

Dickie's blonde head bobbed to the surface. He was swept by the current into the deep water at the heart of the pool, and then went under again. It was a full minute before he bobbed to the surface, another twenty feet downstream. His mouth was wide open. His eyes bulged. He was coughing and sputtering and his face was blotched with purple.

As Dickie slowly drew nearer, Willows saw that the corpse of the girl was only a length behind him. It was Rossiter's case; Willows decided it was only fair to let him have the body. He moved a little to his left, towards Dickie. The water was only waist-deep, but Dickie was too far gone to stand upright.

Willows braced himself. Dickie was floundering, barely managing to keep his head up. His skin was white, pebbled. There was a wild look in his eye. Willows reached out, and got his arms around Dickie's chest. He was surprised to see that Dickie had not let go of the saw. He started moving backwards, hauling Dickie and the chain-saw out of the water and up on the beach. The steel blade of the saw clattered on the rocks. Dickie's teeth were chattering, too. He was shivering uncontrollably.

"You okay?" Willows asked, crouching down next to him.

Dickie didn't seem to hear the question. His eyes were on Rossiter.

Willows stood up. He went over and unrolled the portable stretcher. Rossiter struggled with the body. It was stiff and ungainly, cold as a block of carved ice. Finally he got a grip under the girl's armpits. Her heels left parallel grooves in the sand and gravel as he dragged her out of the water.

"Give me a hand getting her on the stretcher," Rossiter said to Willows. He had seen right away that Dickie wasn't going to be any help.

Willows grasped the girl's ankles. Her flesh was soft and pulpy. She was much heavier than he had expected. Together, he and Rossiter lowered the naked body on to the stretcher. There was a tattoo high up on the inside of the forearm, a smudge of blue that was distorted by the swollen skin.

"What the hell is that?" said Rossiter.

Willows knelt for a closer look. "A Smurf," he said.

"A what?"

"Smurf. Little cartoon character. Don't you ever watch television on Sunday mornings?"

"Not if I can sleep in."

Willows found himself staring at the girl. She would have been very pretty. Embarrassed, he looked away.

Dickie's close-cropped hair lay flat on his head. He fiddled with his moustache. Water dripped from his shirt and blue jeans. He leaned over and hit the chainsaw with the heel of his hand. "I'm going to have to strip this fucker right down to the frame," he said. "Wash all the parts in gasoline, wipe 'em down with an oily rag. Replace the gaskets and probably the wiring."

Rossiter was getting into his trousers. "Life is damn hard," he said. "But death is a whole lot worse."

Dickie ignored him. He ground the toe of his boot into the gravel and pointed at the corpse. His hand shook but he didn't try to steady it. "That's Naomi Lister. Her dad runs the Chevron station down by the highway."

"I don't think I recognize her," Rossiter said.

"She left town a little over a year ago. Went down to Vancouver."

Willows gave Rossiter an enquiring look.

"I've only been stationed here six months," Rossiter

explained. To Dickie, he said, "What'd she do down in the city?"

"How should I know?" Dickie said. He climbed unsteadily to his feet, took a few steps away from them, and threw up.

Willows stared upstream, past the white froth of water and the curving black bulk of the huge egg-shaped boulder. He looked at Rossiter, and Rossiter nodded. They were both thinking that the girl had probably taken off her clothes to go swimming, that if she had, the clothes had to be up there somewhere.

"Jack and I are going to take a little stroll," Rossiter said to Dickie's hunched back.

Dickie made a gagging sound.

Half a mile upstream, they came upon an overgrown logging road and a crumbling corduroy bridge made of cedar logs. The disused road was little more than two faint parallel depressions in the grass. What made it easy to see was the absence of large trees. There were tread marks and torn soil where a four-wheel drive vehicle with a short wheelspan had braked hard. Willows found traces of oil, a few small globules of heavy grease.

The girl's neatly folded clothes were in the fork of a wild cherry near the bridge on the far side of the stream. Willows saw the bright orange tanktop first, and then the white shorts and white tube socks, neatly folded over the running shoes.

Rossiter took the clothing down out of the tree. A pair of white cotton panties with a pattern of little red strawberries fell lightly to the grass. Rossiter picked them up. He went through the pockets of the white shorts, and found three twenty-dollar bills wrapped tightly round a driver's licence and a small black and white photograph. The picture was a head and shoulders shot of a boy in his early teens. His eyes were a very pale grey. The teeth were large, so white that they looked over-exposed.

Rossiter flicked the plastic laminate of the driver's licence with his index finger. "Dickie was right," he said. "Naomi Lister it is."

Rossiter handed the licence to Willows. It was the girl in the river, all right. The licence had been issued two months earlier, on her sixteenth birthday. She had been restricted to driving vehicles with an automatic transmission, and was required to wear corrective lenses.

"You notice she was wearing an engagement ring?" Rossiter said.

"Yeah, I saw it."

"What do you think happened up here, have we got a crime of passion, or what?"

"If I had to guess, I'd say she and whoever drove her up here went for a swim. And she banged her head on a rock, and he panicked. Or maybe he was off in the woods somewhere, wandering around. Maybe he never knew she was in trouble and still has no idea what happened to her."

"If she was with her fiancé, and the death was an accident, wouldn't he have reported the fact that she was missing?"

Willows indicated the small black and white picture. "Be nice to know who he is, wouldn't it?"

"Looks to me like it came from one of those automatic machines."

"Maybe her parents can help you."

"You like to be in on that?"

"Not particularly," said Willows. He handed the driver's licence back to Rossiter. It was a gesture of rejection.

Rossiter tucked the licence and the money and the picture away in his shirt pocket. "We better get back down to the meadow," he said. "That pilot gets paid by the hour."

9

Junior caught a CP Air redeye out of Vancouver International. The plane was almost empty. Junior sat down in an aisle seat over the wing, where he couldn't see the ground even if he forgot and looked out the window.

The plane touched down at LAX at one o'clock in the morning. It took Junior a couple more hours to make the drive down the coast to Felix's beachfront mansion. By the time he hit the sack it was almost four o'clock. At five, Felix and Misha dragged him out of bed to watch the latest shuttle launch. At ten minutes past five, with the three of them sitting in front of the Sony and the first pale light of day seeping hesitantly in through the windows, the flight was cancelled.

Junior mumbled something about going back to bed, but Felix would have none of it. He and Misha had been up all night, smoking a little and drinking a lot. He had his second wind, and he was feeling full of beans. The idea of a picnic breakfast on the beach suited him just fine.

Misha went into the kitchen to prepare the food.

Felix punched through the channel selector to see what was on, and then used the remote control to turn off the TV. Junior was sprawled out on the chesterfield, his eyes half-closed. Felix went over and sat down beside him and patted him on the knee. "It's good to have you back, kiddo."

Junior yawned.

"Been a long night, huh?"

"Yeah."

"Later on, when you're feeling a little more energetic, you'll have to tell me how it went. Okay?"

"Sure," said Junior.

Junior closed his eyes. Felix sat there on the edge of the chesterfield, looking fondly down at him, until Misha came back into the room. She was carrying a wicker basket, holding it awkwardly with both hands. She staggered across the room and dropped the basket on Junior's lap. Junior grunted. The basket looked heavy, and it was a lot heavier than it looked.

They went out of the house, past the patio and the sixty-foot pool, down the long sloping lawn towards the ocean. There were thick wooden planks on weathered poles and a series of narrow wooden steps to get them past the fragile, crumbling dunes. Felix had made a side trip to the kitchen to grab a couple of bottles of Kirin beer from the fridge. He and Misha drank steadily as they stumbled along through the débris at the high-tide line, heading south towards San Diego, giggling like a couple of kids as they clumsily tried to avoid the hiss and rumble and froth of the incoming surf. Junior kept himself occupied by watching Misha's small pointed breasts bouncing around under her halter top. With maddening frequency, Felix tripped himself up and fell full-length and without apparent resistance, his ancient wrinkled face turning into a mask of fine white sand. Resentfully, Junior rinsed him off with hatfuls of ocean while Misha poured Kirin beer over both of them.

As soon as he could see again, Felix got right back at it. Grinning and laughing and reaching out to slap ass, he chased Misha up and down the beach.

Splat! Another face full of sand.

Junior plodded along behind them, his shoulders hunched. He made a point of keeping his distance. It felt as if Misha had filled the wicker basket with anvils. His Colt .357 Magnum with the ribbed and ventilated nine-inch barrel kept rubbing against his hipbone, chafing his skin and forcing him to walk with a crablike sideways shuffle he knew must make him look like a fool. He squinted at the orange ball of the sun, balanced unnaturally on the convex rim of the horizon. Although he had grown up in southern California, he somehow had never managed to adjust to the weather. He wiped sweat from his eyes, and found himself wondering what the weather was like back in Vancouver. Raining, probably.

Up ahead, Felix didn't so much stop walking as simply decide to sit down in mid-stride. When Junior caught up with him, he said, "This looks as good a spot as any. Let's eat."

Misha had folded a fringed tartan blanket over the food. Junior helped her spread it out on the sand. Inside the basket there were a dozen tall brown bottles of Kirin beer, a whole roast chicken, a loaf of brown bread shaped like an iron from the European bakery at Laguna Beach, a thick crystal bowl full of cherry tomatoes, a foot-long English cucumber, and a sterling silver setting for six in a mahogany box. No wonder Junior's back ached. He sat down with his back to the ocean and the rising sun, and took off his shoes. He yawned hugely, making a lot of noise.

Misha quartered the chicken. She sliced up the loaf as neatly as a machine. Felix cracked open three bottles of Kirin beer. He and Misha began to eat, Felix whuffling and snorting like a pig, making a lot of noise.

Junior had eaten three cold roast beef dinners on the plane. He wasn't hungry. He passed the time seeing how thin he could slice the cucumber. The knife was sharp, and he had a steady hand. Wheels as limp as tissue-paper and almost as transparent as glass fell one after another into his lap. Misha and Felix watched him raptly as they ate. After a little while Junior became aware of all the attention he was getting. He lost his concentration, cut deeply into the ball of his thumb. Blood welled up, spilled across his cupped palm. Nobody said anything. Junior sucked at his wound. When the bleeding had finally stopped he looked up and saw that Misha had fallen asleep with her mouth open and that Felix was staring sightlessly out at the ocean, as if mesmerized by the steady pounding of the waves.

Junior drank some beer. He watched Misha's breasts rise and fall as she breathed.

"Ain't she cute?" said Felix.

Junior nodded.

"How's the cut?"

"Just a scratch."

"Let's have a look at it."

Obediently, Junior held out his hand. Felix grabbed the thumb and squeezed hard. A single fat globule of bright red blood appeared. Felix nodded thoughtfully, and let go.

"I've always been quick to congeal," said Junior proudly.

Felix used a wing from the chicken to point at Misha. "We nuked her grandparents," he said.

"What's that again?"

"Her grandparents. World War Two. We nuked 'em."

"And now you're fucking the survivors," said Junior with a grin.

Felix ignored him. "Nagasaki and Hiroshima. Bang! Powie! We vaporized 'em, Junior. Nothing left but shadows on a wall."

"Don't blame me. I wasn't even born."

"I know how old you are," said Felix. "I know how old I am, too." He wriggled his toes in the sand. The sand was cool and it felt good. Firm. Resisting, but yielding. He wriggled deeper. "Tell me what happened last night," he said.

Junior shrugged. "Nothing much. He used the van I told him about. Picked up the kid and took him to a parking lot under an apartment building. Chopped him up and left him and the van in the park."

"What park?"

"Stanley Park. You know Second Beach?"

Felix nodded. "After that, then what?"

"Beats me."

"You see him actually do the killing?"

"No, I didn't. You told me not to get too close."

"Did I?"

"Before he picked up the kid, he stopped off at a grocery store and bought something."

"What?"

"I don't know. Toilet paper, maybe."

"You don't think too much of Mannie, do you?"

"No, I wouldn't say that at all. You need somebody to fetch your newspaper in off the porch, he'd be just about perfect."

Felix finished his beer. He threw the empty bottle towards the water. It skittered across the sand and spun to a stop fifty feet away, end on. "Can you hit that from here?"

"Easy," said Junior, not even bothering to look.

Felix took off his wide-brimmed straw hat and scratched vigorously at the liver spots high up on his forehead, where his hairline used to be. "We got one down and two to go. What I'd like is to let Mannie do the work, and then kill him."

"Fine with me."

"In the meantime, you keep an eye on him. If he starts to get in over his head, then you go right ahead and pull the plug."

"My pleasure," said Junior.

"That is," said Felix with a mocking smile, "if you think you can handle the guy all by yourself."

Junior ripped his shirt in his hurry to get out the Colt. The long barrel slowed him down, but not enough to notice. He thumbed back the hammer. The blade front sight bisected the dark brown disc. He squeezed the trigger. The Magnum went off like a cannon, and a fountain of sand erupted a foot to the right of the bottle.

"Fuck!" shouted Junior. He thumbed back the hammer for a quick second shot.

Misha screamed and jumped up, found herself right in the line of fire.

"Rise and shine!" said Felix cheerfully.

10

The pilot kept the engine running and the power on. Willows pushed the sliding door open and dropped blindly into a maelstrom of dust and small pebbles. Above him the whirling blades spun and clattered, dicing and chopping the air. There was plenty of headroom, but Willows found himself crouching as he trotted down the road towards his Oldsmobile. He was halfway to the car when the helicopter lifted off, the rising scream of the engines and the thud of bruised air pounding down at him in waves.

It was nice to be back on the ground. The short trip down the mountain had been claustrophobic. A puddle of river water had collected under the stretcher, and vibrations transmitted through the metal floor had made the corpse quiver endlessly, as if it was alive and shivering with fear. Willows reflected, not for the first time, how odd it was that the dead always used up so much more space than the living.

Willows unlocked the boot. His service revolver was as he had left it, hidden under the spare tyre and wrapped in a clean white cloth. He put away his gear, shut the boot, got into the car and started the engine. The windscreen, like the rest of the car, was coated in a layer of thick white dust. He turned on the wipers. The blades swept away enough of the dust to make driving possible. The road was deserted. He made a U-turn and accelerated, changed up into second gear. Dust was blown swirling across the painted metal of the bonnet. He hit thirty-five miles an hour and shifted into third.

When the wind of his passage had washed most of the dust from the car, Willows rolled down his side window and then leaned across the seat to roll down the window on the passenger side. Ahead of him, the white road glittered in the sunlight, making him squint.

The same guard was on duty at the gatehouse. He glanced up as Willows drove by, his wounded face registering surprise.

Willows gave him a beep of his horn and kept going. After he'd borrowed the guard's phone to call the RCMP, the man had been all questions. Willows hadn't answered them then, and had no intention of answering them now.

It took him half an hour to drive back to Squamish. He turned off the highway and drove past the Chevron station Dickie had said was owned and operated by Naomi Lister's father. The lights were on inside the office and service bays, but the pumps were dark and the station was closed.

There was a fitful wind blowing up from the Sound, but it wasn't strong enough to drive away the sour smell of the mills. Willows supposed people eventually got used to it, stopped noticing it just as they stopped noticing everything else that was unpleasant. He turned left, following the directions Rossiter had given him. Squamish was a small town. It looked as if it had been that way for a long time and had no future ambitions. He made another left and drove half a block and parked in front of the RCMP detachment, a tidy one-storey lemon brick building crouched behind clusters of white, blue and pink hydrangeas.

Rossiter and Dickie were waiting for him out on the street, lounging purposefully against a blue and white highway cruiser with reinforced bumpers and a light bar crammed with red and blue flashers and white spots. The car was a perfect match for the garden. Somehow Willows doubted if it was deliberate. He rolled up the windows and locked his car. As he got out of the Olds, Rossiter gave him a big smile.

"Welcome to our fair city," Rossiter said.

Willows nodded.

Dickie opened the rear door of the cruiser. Willows got into the car. Dickie slammed the door shut a little harder than should have been necessary. The car smelled faintly of vomit and urine and stale beer and industrial strength cleansers. It was neither better nor worse than being outside.

Dickie slid behind the wheel. Rossiter sat in the passenger seat. Both men were in uniform. Dickie had crossed pistols on his shirtsleeve. From where he was sitting, Willows had a wonderful view of the angry red rash beneath the close-cropped hair at the base of Dickie's stump of a neck. He glanced up, and saw Dickie watching him in the wide rearview mirror.

"Would you mind telling me something," Dickie said. "Would you mind telling me what the hell you're doing here?"

"He's a special guest detective," said Rossiter. "How many times do I have to tell you, for Christ's sake?"

Willows watched the flesh at the back of Dickie's neck rearrange itself in overlapping folds as Dickie twisted in his seat to glare at his partner.

"He found the girl's body," said Rossiter. "If you were her father, wouldn't you want to talk to him?"

"Just don't get in the way," Dickie said into the mirror.

"In the way of what?" said Rossiter. "This isn't a criminal investigation, it's a sympathy call."

"We won't know what happened to her until after the autopsy," said Dickie. "Let's just try to keep that in mind, okay?"

Rossiter half-turned in his seat to face Willows. His left arm lay along the top of the seat. He raised his hand, turned it palm upwards, and let it drop. "You have to understand," he said, "that the most excitement we get around here is when some drunken logger tries to drive his pickup through a fir tree. My friend's been feeling for some time now that his talents are being wasted. He's looking for headlines, and he's hungry."

"Bullshit," said Dickie.

Rossiter grinned. "I admire a man who can get to the crux of his argument with an absolute minimum of words, don't you?"

"Fuck off," said Dickie.

It was a short drive to the Lister house, but to Willows it seemed to take a very long time. He was tired. It had been more than twenty-four hours since he'd last had a hot meal. He needed a shower. And it was exhausting work, listening to the two Mounties chew away at each other. He hoped he wouldn't have to spend too much time at the Lister house. He was looking forward to getting back to the city, back to his own set of problems.

The Lister house was weathered grey clapboard, one and a half storeys high. It was partially screened from the street by a trio of gnarled apple trees, the branches crouching under the weight of clusters of neglected, overripe fruit. Dickie parked the cruiser at the mouth of a dirt driveway. His phone call had caught Naomi Lister's father in the middle of dinner. Lister knew the policemen were coming to see him about his daughter, but he didn't know why.

Rossiter unlocked the rear door for Willows. Dickie had already started to walk away from the car. They skirted a Datsun station wagon with the Chevron logo painted on the side, went down a concrete sidewalk that meandered purposelessly through the trees. Willows noticed that the house needed a new roof, and that the windows were dirty. He followed Dickie and Rossiter up the front steps.

The three men were almost at the top of the steps when the screen door swung open and Lister stepped out on to the porch. Willows guessed his age at about fifty. He was thin, with a full head of unruly white hair and a snub nose that supported the kind of old-fashioned wire-frame glasses favoured by Norman Rockwell. He was wearing clean white coveralls and a checked shirt in three shades of brown, scuffed leather slippers. His eyes were another shade of brown, and the skin around the eyes was slack and lifeless. He looked at Dickie and then at Rossiter and then at Willows and then back to Rossiter. "What's wrong," he said. "What's Naomi done this time?"

Rossiter cleared his throat.

"She stopped paying attention to me the minute her mother died," Lister said in a thin, apologetic voice. He looked at Willows again, and then away.

"Can we go inside for a minute?" Dickie said.

"Sure thing," said Lister. He shuffled over to the porch rail and plucked a dead leaf from a potted begonia. His hand closed on the leaf, crushing it to powder. He brushed his hands together, very slowly, as if it was something he had never done before. Tiny flecks of brown clung to his palms. He wiped his hands vigorously on his overalls and then turned and led his three visitors into the house.

The living-room was dim and warm, crammed with a mix of old and new furniture. It looked as if Lister had recently replaced all the original pieces and then found he lacked the heart to throw them away.

There was a fireplace in the middle of the far wall. The brickwork had been painted a hard, glossy white. The hearth was filled with plastic foliage and a grouping of small ceramic animals. Willows guessed that Lister's wife had created the little tableau, and that since her death the fireplace had become a kind of shrine.

Dickie gestured towards an overstuffed chair. "You want to sit down, Bill?"

Lister shrugged, his shoulders thin and bony under the checked shirt. His pale brown eyes strayed to the large wooden carving that hung over the fireplace and that dominated the room. Christ on the cross. Three feet high, carved out of yellow cedar. The forehead was wide, cheekbones prominent, nose large and forceful. Willows was sure the artist had been a native Indian, probably a Haida. This Christ wasn't languishing on the stake, his eyes cast placidly towards Heaven. He was staring down, glaring at his tormentors, the heavy muscles of his arms and chest and thighs rigid and bulging with tension, his mouth wide open in a snarl of rage.

"I really do think you ought to sit down for a minute," Dickie said.

"Okay," said Lister. He lowered himself into one of the chairs facing the fireplace. "Tell me what happened," he said. "Something bad has happened to her, hasn't it?"

"She's dead," said Dickie flatly. "She appears to have drowned." As he spoke he was staring hard at Lister, watching for his reaction. All at once Willows understood what Rossiter didn't like about him. The man didn't know when to stop being a cop.

"I have to tell you," said Lister, "that I'm not in the least bit surprised."

"Why not?" said Dickie sharply.

Lister didn't seem to hear him. His gaze was focused on a ceramic rabbit hunkered down behind some plastic ivy. He pushed his hands deep into his overall pockets. His shoulders slumped.

"We found her about fifteen miles north of here," Dickie said. "In one of those little creeks up in the mountains. It looked as if she'd gone swimming, maybe hit her head on a rock."

Dickie waited for a response, but none came. He glanced at Rossiter. "There were tread marks from a four-wheel drive near where we found her," he said to Lister. "Do you have any idea who might've driven up there with her?"

"No," said Lister in a quiet voice. He was still staring at the rabbit. Christ was still staring down at all of them.

"Didn't she have a boyfriend?" Dickie said.

"Could have been anybody. Anybody in pants."

Dickie unbuttoned the breast pocket of his shirt. He held out the small black and white photograph of the boy with the pale eyes and wide smile. "You ever see him before, Bill?"

Dickie held the photograph under Lister's nose. Lister glanced at it, shook his head. "Who is he?"

"We don't know. You sure you don't recognize him?"

"I'm sure."

"When Naomi was still living here with you, was there anybody who came around in a four-wheel drive vehicle? Something with a short wheelbase, maybe a jeep?"

"The bastards drove everything from bulldozers to tricycles." Lister spread his arms in a gesture of helplessness. "What was I supposed to do with the girl, chain her to a tree?"

Dickie nodded. "You mind if we take a look in her room?"

"What for?"

"We'd just like to take a look around."

Lister pushed himself to his feet. He glanced vaguely around the room, as if he had forgotten where he was. He gave Willows a polite, fleeting smile.

"Was there anything you wanted to ask me?" Willows said.

"What were you doing up the mountain?"

"Fishing."

"You just stumbled across her by accident, is that it?"

"Pretty much, yes."

"I see," said Lister. He put his hands in his pockets. He took his hands out of his pockets. Then he started diagonally across the room towards an open door leading to a dim, empty hallway. Dickie started after him, and Rossiter followed.

"I'll be out on the porch," Willows said to Rossiter as Rossiter walked by. Rossiter nodded, his face grim. Willows went outside. He took a deep breath, slowly let it out. Behind him, a miniature hydraulic device made the screen door wheeze shut. He started in on the begonia without thinking about what he was doing, tearing away the remaining dead leaves, roughly pruning the dying plant.

After a few minutes Rossiter joined Willows on the porch.

"Let's get the hell out of here."

"What about Dickie?"

"I'll leave the car at the detachment. It's only a couple of blocks. He can walk back."

Rossiter started down the steps. Willows hesitated, and then went after him.

"You got a change of clothes in your car?" asked Rossiter.

"No, why?"

"You can shower and change at my place. We're about the same size. You and me and Katie can go somewhere and grab something to eat. Have a few beers and a good time." He grinned. "Fun, you know what I mean?"

"Thanks anyway, but I think I'd like to get back to the city."

"When d'you last eat, Jack? Before you found the body, I bet. Sometime yesterday afternoon?"

"About then." Willows thought about the long drive through darkness, the empty apartment waiting for him at the end of the ride. "Dinner would be nice," he said.

"Good," said Rossiter.

On the far side of the valley, the mountains cut a jagged chunk out of the setting sun. At the foot of the porch steps, the lengthening shadows of the neglected fruit trees lay heavy on the grass; a complex and tangled web of twisted black lines that seemed to reach out to Willows as he walked towards the car.

Mannie pushed the rewind button. The Hitachi VCR hummed and clicked. Videotape spun from the right wheel to the left. He turned on his TV. It made a crackling sound deep inside, like bacon frying. He turned the sound right down. He'd heard it all before. Nobody said anything. The VCR clicked again. The tape was fully rewound. Mannie pushed the play button. A fuzzy palette of colour coalesced into the face of a young woman with huge brown eyes, masses of auburn hair, a glossy red mouth. Mannie watched the movement of her lips as she read from a slip of paper on her desk.

The camera moved in on the woman. She stopped talking. Her eyes glittered as she stared solemnly into the lens.

On the screen, a free-form blob of polished silver metamorphosed into the radiator of the Econoline van. The camera pulled back, slowly panned the gleaming black flank of the van. It was parked in the lot where he had left it, but now it was cordoned off with lengths of bright yellow plastic tape, and guarded by a quartet of uniformed cops.

The camera cut to a full shot of a thin woman in designer glasses and a pageboy haircut. She was wearing a ruffled grey blouse and a darker grey skirt. There was a wind coming in off the water and she held her microphone in one hand and kept her skirt in place with the other. A gust of wind fanned her hair across her forehead just as she opened her mouth to speak. She brushed the hair back into place with her free hand, and up came the skirt. Nice legs. A little flustered, the woman smiled into the lens. Mannie smiled right back at her. He knew a trouper when he saw one.

The camera moved in on the woman until her glasses and mouth filled the screen. Blah blah blah. The camera pulled back. Inspector Homer Bradley stood to the woman's left, Detective Orwell on her right.

Blah blah blah. Mannie hit the fast forward button. The

machine hummed and whirred and clicked. He hit the stop button, backed up a bit, hit play.

The camera moved unsteadily in on the van. Under the powerful quartz television lights the Econoline was all sparkling chrome, reflected glare, impenetrable black shadows. The angle changed. Mannie guessed the cameraman was holding his unit over his head at arm's length. He saw the lights reflected in the windscreen, a vague distorted human shape.

And then he was inside. Red shag. Silver shards of broken mirror. Pools of black on the bed. Tooth marks on the back of the bucket seat.

Mannie relived those moments when he had snatched quick glimpses of himself in the rearview mirror, his arm a blur, knife and teeth flashing through the red fog. The boy squirming under him, slippery as a fish. The shrill scream of his suit ripping. The jarring thud of steel on bone. Now the images his mind had photographed were interposed upon the flickering image on the screen. The past swallowed the present. The boy grunted. He cried out. He gasped and went limp.

Mannie's brain pushed stop. Rewind. Pause. Fast forward. Play. And the boy died again and again and again.

12

Rossiter's house was three miles out of town and half a mile in from the highway, in the middle of a clearing surrounded by a mix of hardwoods and fir and cedar trees. The house was small, hardly more than a cottage. It had a gently sloping shake roof and a wide front porch. The door and the trim around the mullioned windows was painted a bright, cheerful orange. As Willows got out of his car, the door opened and a tall slim woman wearing a loose grey T-shirt and white shorts stepped out on the porch.

"Katie," said Rossiter, "this is Jack Willows. Jack, I'd like you to meet my one true love."

Katie smiled. She had long black hair and lively green eyes, the kind of skin you saw more often in soap commercials than real life. Willows smiled back. The green eyes studied him for a moment, frankly appraising. Then Katie was turning away, leading them into the cool dimness of the house.

As Willows' eyes adjusted to the light, he found himself standing in the living-room. There was a patterned rug, pine floorboards that gleamed with wax and reflected the grey bulk of a big fieldstone fireplace. He followed Rossiter and Katie across the room, past a sagging chesterfield and a pair of frayed armchairs, a coffee table buried under untidy stacks of *National Geographic*. Rossiter excused himself and ducked through an open doorway into the house's single bedroom. Willows noticed that the bed was made and that there were some yellow flowers in a vase on the bureau. He felt a pang of homesickness, short and sharp.

The bathroom was at the rear of the house, separated from the kitchen by a narrow hallway. Katie handed Willows a stack of towels. "You've got about ten minutes, then you're going to run out of water."

Willows thanked her, squezed into the tiny bathroom and shut the door. There was an old-fashioned pedestal sink, a prefab shower made of plastic panels, and a wicker laundry basket. Willows was standing on the rest of the usable floor space. He balanced the towels on the rim of the sink, stripped, and turned on the shower. Adjusting the spray, he stepped inside. Water swirled around his feet. He yanked the shower curtain shut.

The door swung open. "Clothes," said Rossiter, and quickly shut the door.

There was a bar of soap and a tube of shampoo on a rack built into the shower stall. Willows washed his hair and then used the soap to work up a thick lather. By the time he'd rinsed himself clean the water was starting to run cold. He turned off the taps and pushed back the shower curtain. On top of the laundry hamper Rossiter had left a pale blue shirt, faded jeans, and a pair of undershorts still in the sealed plastic package. Willows dried himself off and got dressed, padded barefoot into the kitchen.

Rossiter was sitting at the table, peeling potatoes. There was an open bottle of beer in front of him. He used the potato peeler to point at the beer and then the refrigerator. "Help yourself."

"Thanks." Willows opened the fridge and took out a bottle of Kootenay Pale Ale, twisted off the cap.

"You mind if we eat here instead of going into town?" said Rossiter.

"No, not at all. Is there anything I can do to help with dinner?"

"Not that I can think of. But if I'm wrong, Katie'll let you know."

Willows pulled out a chair and sat down at the table. He leaned back and sipped his beer, watched Rossiter hack at the potatoes. The back door swung open and Katie came in, her arms full of vegetables from the garden. She glanced quickly at Willows and said, "You look exhausted. Why don't you go stretch out in the living-room?"

Willows hesitated.

"Or would you rather peel spuds?" said Rossiter.

"It's touch and go," said Willows, "but I think I'll take the couch."

He'd finished his beer and read most of a lengthy article on

71

the fate of elephants in Kenya when Katie came into the room. "Dinner is served," she said, and gave him a little bow and offered him her hand.

They drank rough Italian red with potatoes baked in butter and lemon juice, a green salad, thick charbroiled steaks. The meat was dark and grainy. It wasn't beef. Willows, his mouth full, looked up from his plate.

Rossiter had been waiting. He held up his hands on either side of his head, spread his fingers wide. Antlers. Grinning, he pointed out the window towards the mountains.

For dessert they had home-made huckleberry pie and vanilla ice-cream, washed down with stoneware mugs of fresh-ground coffee. When the coffee pot was empty Rossiter brought out a second bottle of wine. They took the wine and their glasses back into the living-room. Katie put a Mozart piano concerto on the turntable. They talked about music, and then Willows told them what he'd learned about elephants in Kenya. The conversation drifted, interspersed with periods of reflective silence that never seemed forced or awkward. Finally Rossiter brought up the shooting, Dickie's deliberate wounding of the unarmed youth. Willows didn't quite know what to say. It all seemed so obvious. Dickie had the law on his side but was morally out to lunch. There was nothing much Rossiter could do but keep a close eye on him. Or resign in protest from the Force.

"You ever have to shoot anybody?" Rossiter asked. He was slurring his words. Willows realized he was drunk.

"A couple of times."

"Twice?"

"Yeah, that's right. Twice."

"I don't know if I could do it," said Rossiter. "It sounds weird, but I just don't know."

"When the time comes, it isn't something you think about. You just react."

"What if you make a mistake, blow somebody away who didn't have it coming? Then what? You ever worry about that?"

Willows smiled politely. "No, I worry about something else."

The level of wine in the bottle slowly dropped, the mullioned windows darkened. Willows yawned widely, and apologized.

72

Katie went out of the room and came back carrying a pillow and sheets, a folded Hudson's Bay blanket. Rossiter stood up, a little unsteady on his feet. He said goodnight and left the room. Katie leaned over and kissed Willows on the cheek, surprising both of them.

Left to himself, Willows made up his bed on the chesterfield. He turned out the lights and undressed in darkness. In the kitchen he could hear dishes being washed, whispered conversation. Katie apparently didn't think Rossiter should have asked Willows if he'd ever shot anybody. Willows couldn't have agreed more.

He closed his eyes, and immediately fell into a deep and dreamless sleep.

He slept twelve hours, and when he woke up the house was empty. There was a message on the kitchen table. Katie was shopping in Squamish, Rossiter was on duty. Willows' clothes were on the line. Willows turned the slip of paper over and wrote a short note of thanks. He went out into the back yard and retrieved his clothes, dressed hurriedly. He didn't want to think about it, but for some reason he wanted to be on his way before Katie got back from her shopping.

He arrived back in the city late in the afternoon. The air in his apartment was warm and stale. He unlocked and slid open the glass door that led to the vestigial balcony. There was a faint breeze coming in from the ocean; he could smell fish and chips and sun-tan oil.

In the kitchen he put the kettle on to boil, scooped enough coffee into the filter to make a full pot. There was a loaf of sliced white bread on the counter, the kind that was essentially tasteless but had a shelf-life measured in seasons. He rummaged through the fridge, found a rectangle of cheese and a dozen eggs. He couldn't remember when he'd bought the eggs. The cheese looked all right, though, and there was margarine. He could make a sandwich. The kettle screamed at him. He took it off the burner and poured boiling water over the coffee grounds. He felt deeply depressed, emotionally adrift. Against his better judgement, knowing it was a stupid thing to do but doing it anyway, he went into the bedroom and called his wife.

The phone rang nine times, and then Willows stopped counting. He conjured up a picture of her in the garden, cutting flowers for the Sunday table with an old pair of shears. It had been something her mother did, and now it was a ritual Sheila was trying to instil in their children. Hoping to give them a sense of the continuity of life, he supposed.

When she finally answered, she sounded hurried and out of breath. He imagined her hearing the telephone, saw her drop the big scissors and a gathered handful of white carnations, run across the lawn and up the back porch steps, into the shade and coolness of the house.

He said hello.

There was a pause, a fraction of a moment's silence. Then, "Jack, is that you? I didn't think you were coming back until tomorrow." A gratifying note of concern. "Are you all right?"

"I decided to come back early, that's all." Another pause. "How are you, Sheila?"

"I'm fine, just fine."

"Annie and Sean?"

"Perfect. Listen, are you sure you're okay?"

"Positive. Never better. Tell me, Sheila, were you out in the garden just now?"

"No, why?"

"You're huffing and puffing, that's why."

Sheila laughed. A bit self-consciously, Willows thought.

"I was in the den. Flat on my back in front of the television. Doing sit-ups. I rented a Jane Fonda tape, can you believe it?"

"Everybody's doing it," said Willows. He almost added, *it's a fad*, but stopped himself in time.

"How was the fishing?"

"Not as good as the beans."

"Work?"

"It's always the same. It never changes." What had made him say that? It was like a declaration of war, a statement of intent, inflexible and unyielding.

They talked about the garden for a little while, the annual proliferation of weeds. Willows was about to say his goodbyes when Sheila reminded him that the children were scheduled to spend the next weekend with him. Was that still on? He assured her that it was. She told him to take care of himself, her words

74

widely spaced, as if deliberately letting him know that she had all the time in the world to ramble on. Willows said goodbye and hung up, gently cradling the receiver.

The room was very quiet. He realized that during his absence the alarm had run down. Setting it by his watch, he wound the mainspring tight.

The telephone rang, the sound unnaturally loud and shrill. Willows picked it up, assuming that Sheila had wanted to add a postscript.

"I thought you weren't getting back until tomorrow," said Claire Parker.

"Then why did you bother to phone?"

"I had a hunch. What you'd think of as intuition. It happens all the time, as a matter of fact."

"Like acid indigestion."

"You interested in a murder case that's a little out of the ordinary?"

"Where are you?"

"Main Street. I've got an appointment with Bradley in half an hour."

"See you there," said Willows.

Parker hung up. Willows sat on the edge of his rented bed with the dead telephone in his hands. He never missed his weekends with Annie and Sean. Why had Sheila found it necessary to check on his plans? Was it because she had plans of her own? And not that it was any of his business, but why had she suddenly felt compelled to start working out with Jane Fonda? Just exactly what was she getting in shape for?

Willows felt a stab of jealousy, a small, sharp spasm of fear.

13

Junior wandered aimlessly through the big house, his hands in his pockets and his mind a blank. He hit a cross-current and realized he was hungry, followed his nose into the kitchen. A skinny kid in a Kung-Fu outfit was hunched over the stove. One of Misha's relatives. Impossible to say how old he was – not that it mattered. He was using a big wooden spoon to push a colourless mix of noodles and small bits of stringy meat around a stainless steel wok. Junior, peering over the kid's shoulder, decided the food smelled a whole lot better than it looked.

Turning away from the stove, Junior yanked open the refrigerator door. He was in luck. There was a big plate of crab sandwiches left over from lunch, and an open bottle of Robert Mondavi Fumé Blanc. Junior pulled the cork with his teeth. The sandwiches were tiny, without crusts, and had been cut in weird shapes. He ate six of them, washing each one down with a good healthy slug of wine.

There was nobody in the oak-panelled den or in the living or dining-rooms. Nobody in the can. Nobody out by the tennis court or sixty-foot pool. Junior made his way back through the house to the front porch. He scratched his sunburned nose and peered out at the ocean. After a while he went upstairs, to the top floor of the house. He was wearing a pair of white leather Hi-Toppers, baggy white shorts and a surfer shirt covered with palm trees and hand grenades that at first glance looked like pineapples. The Hi-Toppers made no sound on the thick wall-to-wall, but Felix was alerted by the click of the latch and his rheumy grey eyes were focusing on the door as Junior opened it.

Junior grinned. "Hey there, Felix. Hope I didn't wake anybody up."

Felix wiped a smear of saliva from his chin. He yawned and rubbed the sleep from his eyes. Junior watched him struggle to sit up, made no attempt to help as Felix's bony arms and sagging flesh sank into the downy berm of the pillows. Felix's dentures were in a Duralex glass on the night-table beside the bed. He spilled a little water getting them out of the glass and into his mouth. When his teeth were firmly in place he gave Junior a big, dripping smile.

"Nice to see you, big fella!"

"I don't think I much care for that thirty-weight tone of voice of yours," said Junior. But he stepped inside the room and shut the door.

"Quiet!" hissed Misha.

Junior gave her a look like she was something he'd found wedged between his two front teeth. She was lying on the far side of Felix's monstro canopied four-poster, watching a Japanese movie on a big screen suspended from the ceiling at the other end of the room. She had a bulky pair of Sony headphones clamped on her head and there was a young girl sleeping in the crook of her arm. The girl was lying on her side and from where Junior was standing he couldn't see her face. He wondered if he knew her. The way Felix and Misha ran through them, it was pretty unlikely.

"Live from Osaka," said Felix, waving a mottled hand at the screen. "Up on the roof I got one of those big white fibreglass things with a wire sticking out of the middle." He paused for a minute, thinking hard, and then pounded a pillow in apparent frustration. "There's a name for the fuckin' thing, but I can't remember what it is."

"A fuckin' dish," said Junior.

"I got stuff coming in from all over the globe, they bounce it down at me from satellites. American ones, French and Russian and German. Even the Italians got one up there." He chuckled. "I can watch Clint Eastwood westerns all day long if I feel like it."

"Terrific."

"And all the sports you can imagine. Not just baseball and football and hockey and shit like that. You ever heard of jai alai?"

"You forgot to mention lawn bowling," said Junior. He drank some Robert Mondavi and wiped his mouth with the back of his hand. "Who's the girl?"

77

Felix shrugged. The tangled sheets were down around the girl's waist, bunched at the curving swell of her hips. Her skin was very dark, and Junior had assumed she was yet another of Misha's numerous relatives, or maybe the friend of a friend. But now Felix gave the sheet a yank, pulling it down to her knees, and Junior found himself staring at a tiny white triangle of untanned flesh. He wondered what beach the girl hung out at, where it was in California you could get away with wearing a bikini that small. He swallowed.

"You like?" said Felix. He tugged at the girl's smooth brown shoulder, rolling her over on her back. She had small breasts, large nipples. Her eyes were closed and her lips were slightly parted. Junior could just make out the tip of her tongue, pink and wet. He watched Felix slide his old man's hand down and across her smooth flat stomach, explore her belly button with the tip of his little finger.

Push hard.

The girl's eyelashes fluttered. She muttered something thick and incomprehensible, and tried to roll back over on her side.

"She thinks you're real cute," Felix translated. "In fact, she can hardly keep her eyes off you."

The girl started snoring. Felix pinched her nostrils shut. Without waking, she slapped weakly at his hand. Junior watched her breasts jiggle.

"You know what happened this afternoon?" said Felix. "I tuned my satellite dish in on the fair city of Vancouver, Canada. And you know what? It seems a girl called Naomi Lister drowned herself to death in some creek about sixty miles out of the city."

"No shit," said Junior, sounding bored.

"So now what's your opinion of Mannie Katz, huh?"

"My opinion is I got a whole box of wadcutters with his name on 'em. Big soft-nosed bullets that mushroom on impact, knock chunks off him big enough for hamburger patties."

Felix grinned. "What a thing to say!"

"I'd like to stick my Colt in his eye and pull the trigger."

"You're a tough cookie, Junior. I'll say that much for you."

"Blow his fucking head right off."

Felix patted the bed. "You need an outlet for all that

repressed anger," he said. "Why don't you come on over and join us?"

Junior finished the last of the wine. It tasted warm and fruity. "How old is she?"

"Sweet sixteen."

"Bullshit."

"No, really. She showed Misha her driver's licence. She's from Ignacio."

"What, the Air Force base?"

"Her daddy's in Germany. He's a button pusher. Got himself one of those big Pershing missiles."

"Let's hope he doesn't get mad and point the fucking thing at us."

Felix smiled condescendingly. The only time Junior made jokes was when he was nervous, and they both knew it. He patted the bed again. "Why don't you get naked and shake hands with our new friend." He smiled. "I think you'll find she's got a very good grip."

"When she's conscious, anyway."

"Hey, why be so picky?"

"I'm in a picky mood."

"Pick on me," said Misha.

Junior realized that the movie had ended and that another one was about to begin. He looked at Felix. Felix stared unblinkingly at him, his dark and glittery lizard's eyes giving away nothing. Junior let the empty wine bottle drop to the rug. He unbuttoned his shirt and took it off, tugged at his belt, unzipped his fly. The moppet from Ignacio was awake and all three of them were watching him, now. He kicked out of his Hi-Toppers. There was a network of blue veins in Felix's drooping eyelids. Junior paused.

"Don't worry about it," said Felix. "All I'm gonna do is watch."

"Where have I heard that before?"

Felix rolled his eyes.

Junior let the shorts drop. His penis was limp and accordioned, his testicles drawn up snug. He moved towards the bed, threw himself full length on the girl from Ignacio, kissed her mouth.

79

Misha's tongue fluttered in his ear. She whispered something to him in Japanese.

"Haven't I seen you somewhere before?" Junior said to the girl.

Misha giggled, hiding her mouth behind her hands.

"We found her in L.A.," said Felix. "Slinging quiche in one of those tacky vegetarian joints over on La Cienga."

"No shit," said Junior. "That's just amazing." He kissed the girl again, bit gently on her lower lip. She moaned softly, but he couldn't have said why.

The metallic cricket sound of a power winder intruded. Junior glanced up to find Felix peering at him through a stubby 28mm wide-angle lens. He remembered his anger the first time this had happened, and Felix's solemn advice: If you wanna look good in the sack, kiddo, never stop smiling.

14

Inspector Bradley's office was on the third floor of police headquarters at 312 Main. The room was not large and it contained too much furniture. There was a battered cherrywood desk, a black leather recliner chair, three varnished wooden chairs, and several gunmetal grey filing cabinets. The desk and leather chair were Bradley's personal possessions; signs of his seniority and rank.

There was only one window in the room. It was a small window and it had been painted shut, but it faced north, towards the inner harbour and bluish bulk of the mountains. Reluctantly, Bradley turned away from the picture postcard view. Lowering himself gently into his leather chair, he leaned back and rested his clasped hands on his slightly protruding stomach.

Above him hung a quartet of bare neon tubes suspended from the ceiling by thin chains. There was something wrong with the circuitry, a bad connection somewhere. The lights made a constant buzzing noise that Bradley found impossible to block out when he was feeling overworked, tired. The noise was bothering him now, had been pressing in on his nerves all day long. He flipped up the lid of an ornately-carved cedar humidor and selected a cigar. Parker and Willows were sitting in front of him, perched on two of the varnished chairs. He pointed the cigar at Willows and said, "You read the coroner's report, Jack?"

"Yeah, I read it."

"Then I don't have to explain why I look so unhappy, do I?"

Willows didn't bother to answer. Although Bradley looked exactly as glum as always, neither more nor less, Willows wasn't about to say so.

Bradley fished a big wooden kitchen match out of his jacket pocket. He flicked at it with his thumbnail. "Look what we've got," he said. "A whorehouse on wheels, hot-wired with

81

prefabricated alligator clips. Strapped to the steering-wheel, a Timex watch with the crystal smashed and the hands stopped at the probable time of the murder. In the back seat we have a bed and on top of the bed a much-punctured juvenile dressed like a hooker, no I.D."

Bradley chewed on his cigar. "Under the corpse, we find some skin mags and a cash register receipt. And except for the knife sticking out of the victim, that's it. No other physical evidence whatsoever."

He pointed his cigar at Parker. "Claire and Farley Spears were trying to find out where the dirty magazines had come from when Spears came down with the mumps, or whatever the hell it is he's got."

"Chickenpox," said Parker.

Bradley ignored her. He flashed a dazzling smile at Willows. "How was the vacation?"

"Great," said Willows without enthusiasm.

"Well, it's over now, Jack. So let's get out on the street and hit that grindstone, okay?"

When Parker and Willows had gone and his office door had swung shut behind them, Bradley struck at the match again, and this time it flared into life. He touched the outer edge of the flame to his cigar, concentrating hard. When he had the cigar burning evenly, he blew out the match and tossed it into the metal wastebasket beside his desk. The lid of the humidor was still up. He flipped it shut and pushed the little box away from him. Smoke drifted upwards towards the harshly buzzing lights. He rubbed the back of his neck and then yanked open the top drawer of his desk, looking for his bottle of aspirins.

Bradley lost aspirins the way other people lost ballpoint pens. They were never where he left them. Never! Frustrated, he slammed the drawer shut. He couldn't understand it.

It was as if the goddamn things had legs.

15

There is a phenomenon known to the medical profession in general and forensic pathologists in particular as "gravitational sinking". The phrase refers to the areas of discoloration, huge dark bruises, that gradually appear on an unattended corpse and are a consequence of blood slowly settling to the lower areas of a body.

When the morgue attendant rolled open the stainless steel drawer containing the mortal remains of the unidentified white male, preliminary case and tag number 19H88, whom Parker had discovered in the back of the stolen Econoline van, Willows saw immediately that there was very little evidence of gravitational sinking. This came as no surprise, since he'd already examined Mel Dutton's Polaroid shots of the body and the inside of the van. There had been blood everywhere, hard and shiny as a carapace in the glare of the camera's flash. Of the seventy-two stab wounds that had been inflicted on the victim, three had severed major arteries. The dying boy had pumped himself dry with the final beats of his heart; there was not enough blood left in his body for gravitational sinking to occur.

Willows leaned forward and pulled down the pale blue rubberized sheet that covered the body, exposing the coroner's sternum-to-pubis Y-shaped incision and the hurried, looping, Raggedy-Ann stitches left by a busy intern.

During the first few hours following the death of a human being, the temperature of the body drops by about three degrees per hour. Then, gradually, the rate of heat loss slows until it is one degree or less per hour. The boy had now been dead more than thirty-six hours. His corpse was as cold as it would get during his stay in the morgue: 38 degrees Fahrenheit and holding steady. Willows picked up a hand. Death reached up at him through the network of nerve endings in his fingertips. He twisted the wrist, slowly turning the arm back and forth under the shadowless white glare of the lights.

There was a deep, wedge-shaped chunk of flesh cut out of the boy's forearm, and on the bottom edge of the cut, a tiny half-circle of blue. Willows examined the arm carefully, and then let it drop. It hit the stainless steel drawer with a dull, meaty thud.

"Looking for anything in particular?" said Parker.

"Yeah, you know what a Smurf is?"

Parker nodded, smiling. "A little cartoon eunuch that looks like a Pillsbury Dough Boy, except it's bright blue."

"A fan, are you?"

"Sometimes on Saturday I go over to my sister's for breakfast. She cooks the pancakes while I watch Smurfs on television with her little girl."

Willows leaned forward so he could look directly down at the boy's face. The eyes were pale green. He pulled back the upper lip, exposing the same large white teeth he'd seen in the black and white picture he and Rossiter had found in Naomi Lister's shorts.

The rubberized sheet made a faint whispering sound as he pulled it back over the boy's body. Spooky. He let the sheet drop. It billowed like a sail in the wind and then settled snugly around the corpse.

"You know Eddy Orwell pretty well, don't you?" said Parker unexpectedly.

"I've spent some time with him."

"Friday night, at that restaurant in the park, he was really nervous. As if he had something on his mind, you know what I mean?"

"No," said Willows, "I'm not sure I do."

"When I hit that Econoline van, pulling out of the parking lot . . ." Parker paused. She stared down at the outline of the body. "You know what I thought when I saw that kid lying there?"

"No, what?"

"That it was a joke, some kind of stupid prank. I thought Eddy Orwell and his dumb-ass pals from vice had paid the kid a few dollars, chipped in for a bottle of ketchup, and were squatting out there in the bushes laughing their heads off at my expense."

Willows walked around Parker to the foot of the stainless

steel drawer. A large brown paper bag was nestled between the boy's ankles. He opened the bag and turned it upside down, shook out a pair of Nikes, socks, a banana-coloured shirt and white linen pants. Flakes of dried blood fell on the rubberized sheet as he went through the clothing. He took out his pen and notebook, and wrote down sizes and brand names.

"Then," continued Parker, "I realized I was looking at real blood, the body of a kid so young he wasn't even out of his teens. And do you know what my reaction was? Anger. I was furious, and I took it out on poor Eddy!"

Willows pushed the clothes back in the brown paper bag. He gave the drawer a push. It was on nylon rollers, and slid shut easily and silently.

"The guy spent a small fortune buying me dinner," said Parker, "and I made him feel like a jerk."

Willows smiled. "Sometimes when Sean fell down and hurt himself, I'd get angry at him, mad because he'd been so careless. Of course, the real reason I was upset was because my son was in pain and there was nothing I could do about it. You still mad at Eddy?"

"No, I want to nail the bastard who killed that kid."

"And the kid's girlfriend," said Willows.

Parker stared at him.

Willows started towards the double doors with their small panes of frosted and wired safety glass. "Let's go get a cup of coffee, Claire, and I'll tell you all about it."

At the Denny's on Burrard a smiling waiter with a round face crammed with pale orange freckles led them to a horse-shoe-shaped booth next to the window. Willows ordered coffee and a jelly doughnut. Parker thought about it for a long time, and then asked for a pot of lemon tea.

Out in the bright, sun-splashed street, a tourist bus cruised slowly past. The bus was a big fire-engine red double-decker imported from London. Parker squinted into the glare as shards of light bounced off the two rows of polished windows that ran the full length of the vehicle. Many of the people in the bus were staring at her as if they had never seen anyone eat at a Denny's before, and she was the advertised highlight of the tour. She repressed an urge to favour them with a regal wave of her hand. She knew Willows well enough to be certain that he'd consider such a gesture badly misplaced.

The waiter came back, interrupting her line of thought. Parker nodded her thanks. She lifted the lid of her teapot and looked inside, dropped a thick slice of lemon into her cup. She liked her tea hot and strong. She filled her cup and then used her spoon to retrieve the slice of lemon, and ate the pulp.

"Vitamin C," she said to Willows, who was watching her from across the table.

Willows poured cream into his coffee. He used his knife and fork to dice his doughnut. It was a mannerism he had picked up a long time ago, from a detective named Norm Burroughs. The first time Burroughs had eaten a jelly doughnut, Willows had thought he was trying in some misdirected way to be genteel. But Burroughs was simply practical – taking care of his clothes.

When he'd finished eating, Willows signalled the waiter for more coffee, and dabbed at his mouth with a paper napkin, wiping away a few granules of sugar. He crumpled the napkin into a ball and threw it on the table. Then he told Claire Parker about the drowned girl, the blue tattoo of a Smurf she'd had on her arm, and the three twenty-dollar bills wrapped around the black and white snapshot of the boy now lying coldly in the morgue.

"What do the Mounties think?" said Parker when Willows had finished.

"Naomi Lister went swimming and bumped her head on a rock and drowned. Death by misadventure. Nice and simple. No muss, no fuss."

"They think she was all by herself up there on the mountain?"

"There's an old overgrown road up there, a Forest Services fire-break. We found tyre tracks."

"She was with a boyfriend, right?"

"That was the supposition."

There had been two fat slices of lemon on Parker's plate. She picked up the second slice and bit into it and chewed slowly, savouring the bitterness of the fruit. She swallowed and said, "You think her boyfriend drowned her, and then came down to the city and killed the kid?"

"No," said Willows, "I don't."

Parker waited a moment, and then said, "Did she actually have a boyfriend? Are the Mounties looking for anyone in particular who she might've gone swimming with?"

"Her father said she went out with anybody in pants. But nobody in particular. He also mentioned that she'd been living down here in Vancouver for the past year or so."

"You mean in the city?"

"Yeah, right."

"What was she doing, did he know?"

"Nope." Willows used the tines of his fork to scrape some jelly from his plate. "But whatever it was, she was making a lot of money at it."

"Prostitution," said Parker firmly. "If we ask around on the street, we'll soon find out who her friends were."

"That'd be nice," said Willows. "Because I'm kind of in a hurry to solve this one." He flagged the waiter and asked him for a copy of the Yellow Pages.

"And more hot water," said Parker, "and a couple more slices of lemon."

When the waiter returned he was carrying the phone book, a pot of fresh coffee, and a large whole lemon on a plate. He served the lemon to Parker, and then filled Willows' cup. Willows added cream. Parker picked up the lemon. She bent her arm at a ninety-degree angle and crooked her wrist, let go of the lemon. It dropped and hit her bicep. At the moment of impact she flexed her muscles. The lemon rebounded upwards, back into her open hand. She dropped the lemon again, and kept dropping and catching it while Willows turned the flimsy pages of the phone book.

"What are you looking for?" she said at last.

Willows' index finger moved down one page and up the next, and then stopped. He tore out the page and folded it up and put it away in his pocket, then shut the phone book. "There are only three tattoo parlours in the entire city," he said. "Two of them are on Hastings, the third's in the six hundred block Davie."

Parker nodded. Many of the downtown core's teenage hookers hung out on Davie. Although neither she nor Willows had

87

much faith in coincidence, it was hard not to feel a little optimistic about this one.

"I'll phone the Squamish detachment and get them to wire down a photograph of the Smurf tattoo on Naomi Lister's arm," said Willows.

"I doubt if it'll do much good," said Parker. "Do these tattoo joints keep customer records? It's all walk-in trade and cash over the counter."

"You're probably right," Willows conceded. "But it won't take long to check it out."

"The street's something else again. We flash the morgue snaps around, it might get us somewhere. Two dead hookers should give us a certain amount of leverage with the survivors."

Willows glanced at his watch. The street didn't start to wake up until ten or eleven – they were in for a late night.

Parker, reading his mind, said, "What do you want to do in the meantime, have you got any plans?"

"I plan to buy some chewing-gum," said Willows. He reached for the bill. "My treat, Claire."

Parker thanked him, but not with a great deal of enthusiasm. Next time it would be her turn to catch the tab. Willows had a knack for changing the price of a pot of tea into a free three-course meal.

There were eight grocery stores and one supermarket in the five-block strip between Broughton and Burrard, each store squeezed in among dozens of night clubs, sex shops, and fast-food joints. Seven of the eight stores sold the kind of magazines that had been found in the back of the Econoline van. Willows and Parker walked down one side of Davie and back up the other, buying a single pack of sugar-free gum at each of the stores, asking for and receiving a cash-register receipt every time they made a purchase.

The receipt from the sixth store they visited matched the Xerox copy of the one they'd found in the van. The receipt was stamped on a thin white slip of paper measuring two by two-and-a-half inches. At the top of the slip there were four short vertical bars and then a space and two more bars. Below the two bars there was blank paper, an asterisk followed by the price of the gum, and then a capital "A" and a plus mark. One line down, the asterisk and the price were repeated, but this time the price was followed by a capital "T" and a four-digit number and, finally, the day's date.

Willows pulled out his worn leather wallet and flashed his gold shield. The girl behind the counter was Chinese, in her early twenties. She looked startled, and then confused, and then a little bit guilty. It was a typical response – none of the expressions that had fleetingly crossed her face had meant a thing, and Willows and Parker both knew it. Parker gave the girl a reassuring smile. She introduced herself and Willows, and asked the girl what her name was.

"Cheryl," said the girl. She hadn't stopped staring at Willows' shield. He folded his wallet and put it back in his pocket.

"Last Friday," said Parker, "someone came in here and bought four sex magazines." She named the magazines. "Do you remember the sale?"

"I'm sorry, no," said the girl. For emphasis, she shook her head. Her ponytail waggled from side to side. "What did he look like," she said. And then, "Was it a man or a woman?"

"We don't know," said Willows. "Probably a man, but we can't be sure."

"What time was he here?"

"In the evening. Why, what difference does it make?"

"We open at ten in the morning, and don't close until midnight." She paused for a moment, thinking, and then said, "I think it would be better if you talked to my grandmother." She locked the cash-register and dropped the key in her pocket. "I'll go and see if she's awake. I'll be right back, okay."

"Sure," said Parker.

"Gum?" said Willows, offering the pack.

Parker shook her head, no.

Willows stripped the wrapper from three pink sticks and popped them into his mouth, chewed fastidiously.

"Does it taste as good as it sounds?" said Parker.

"That's the traffic you hear, not me chewing."

The grandmother was wearing a shapeless black cotton dress and black canvas running shoes. Her hair was tied in a bun, and her skin was smooth and tight except in the area of her mouth and eyes, where it had the texture of finely-woven cloth. Willows had no idea how old she was, but he was certain that she was much older than anyone he'd ever met before. He gave her his name and Parker's, and showed her his badge. She examined it carefully, then nodded and gave him a quick, shy smile, a glimpse of many gold fillings. Cheryl brought out a folding stool, and helped her grandmother sit down, taking her weight, guiding her.

"She speaks very little English," Cheryl said. "I will translate for you, if you like."

"Would you ask her if she remembers selling the magazines," said Willows.

"Yes, I have already done that. She says she remembers very clearly."

"Can she describe the customer?"

"It was a man," said Cheryl. "You must understand that she is embarrassed to discuss this, because of the subject-matter of the magazines." She turned to her grandmother and spoke in rapid-fire Mandarin, a blur of consonants.

The old woman was about to answer when two small children, a boy with his sister in tow, came up to the counter clutching a grape popsicle and a grimy fistful of small coins. The murder investigation ground to a halt while the sale was rung up. Willows volunteered to split the popsicle in half, and was viewed with a mixture of suspicion and alarm.

The children left, and the grandmother resumed speaking. She spoke for several minutes, pausing frequently to catch her breath, and to think. When she finally stopped talking, the girl asked her a number of questions and then turned to Willows and Parker.

"She thinks the man you are looking for came into the store a few minutes after nine o'clock. She says he was not very tall, perhaps five foot eight inches. He was balding. He wore four large gold rings on his right hand, and three more gold rings on his left hand. He had blue eyes. Very pale. Also watery. As if he was just about to begin crying or had just stopped crying. But he did not seem sad. In fact he was very cheerful."

"Can your grandmother tell us what the man was wearing?"

"A dark green suit. No jacket. A white shirt that was very rumpled, in need of ironing. And a very colourful tie. Red, blue and orange."

"Did she notice his shoes?"

"He was not wearing shoes. He was barefoot, and he walked with a limp."

Willows glanced up from his notebook. "A limp? Is she sure about that?"

A quick exchange of Mandarin, short and sharp.

"It was his right foot that was bothering him."

The grandmother frowned at Willows as Cheryl spoke. Willows repressed a smile. "Good," he said, and made a note in his book. "You said he was not very tall. What about his body shape? Was he fat, thin . . . ?"

"My grandmother says the man's shoulders were very narrow. His hips were wide, his legs short and thick. She says he looked like a pear balanced on two sausages."

Willows smiled. The old lady's eyes were alight with intelligence. He suspected that her command of the language was a lot better than her granddaughter thought.

"How did he pay for the magazines?"

"With two twenty-dollar bills. They were brand new."

"Is it possible these bills might still be in the cash-register?"

The girl shook her head. "We do a night deposit as soon as we close. Anything larger than a ten goes to the bank."

Willows had a few more questions. Did the man have any visible scars? Speak with an accent? Did he have any unusual mannerisms? He didn't think they'd get much more out of the old woman, but that was all right, because they already had more than he'd hoped for. He asked the girl if they could use the telephone to call for a police artist and an Identikit. While Parker was dialling, Willows said, "Your grandmother surprises me. Does she remember all her customers so well?"

"My grandmother was frightened of this man," said Cheryl after another short conversation in Mandarin.

"Why?"

"He stole a package of breath mints from the rack by the cash-register. She was afraid that he might try to rob her."

"Why didn't she call the police?"

"He didn't realize she had seen him take the mints. She charged him for them without telling him, so nothing was lost."

The grandmother had watched Parker make her call. Willows was willing to bet she'd memorized the number. She was a real sharpie, one in a million.

So far, all the luck in the case seemed to be running his way.

16

Early the next morning, the skinny kid Junior had seen in the kitchen staggered in carrying a big breakfast tray with folding legs. Misha hopped out of bed long enough to help him get the tray set up, then climbed back in between Junior and Felix.

Misha's plate was covered in small, overlapping, glistening pink horseshoes of raw fish, and the torn leaves of a dark green vegetable Junior had never seen before. He decided that if he offered him a forkful, he'd make the girl from Ignacio choke it down.

The skinny kid went from one side of the bed to the other, his eyes on the ladies as he poured coffee from an ornate sterling pot into bone china cups so thin you could almost see through them.

Junior drank some coffee and nibbled at a piece of whole-wheat toast. He'd been served hash-browns and bacon, and a heap of scrambled eggs made with white wine and a touch of cayenne pepper, but the raw fish and the sound of Felix at the trough had stripped him of his appetite.

"If you aren't going to eat your bacon, can I have it?" said the cute little moppet from Ignacio.

"Sure," said Junior. The girl's shoulder touched his as she leaned towards him to stab at his plate with her fork. Junior slid his hands under the sheet and stroked her hip. "What would your daddy say if he could see you now?"

"My dad's in Germany."

"Yeah, I know." Junior's fingers pushed into the triangular thicket of her pubic hair. "But what would he say, huh?"

The girl smiled. "He's got an awful temper. Just awful."

"Explains why he's riding a Pershing Two. You got to have somebody there who's willing to push that button, right? Otherwise, what's the point?"

"I don't know much about politics," said the girl.

"I love you just the way you are," said Junior. He picked up the sterling silver coffee pot and poured himself a second cup.

"Enjoying your breakfast?" said Felix.

Junior, his mouth full of hot coffee, could only nod.

"That's wonderful. But whatever you do, don't miss your flight."

"What flight?"

"CP 412 out of LAX," said Felix. "You're skedded to lift off in a couple of hours."

"Where am I going, for Chrissake?"

"I want my place in the Properties tuned up." Felix smiled. "I'm thinking of making a run across the border."

"What for?"

"Take the shrouds off the furniture. Open a few windows and let in some fresh air. Fill the pool. Lay in a good supply of food and drink, put a couple buckets of ice-cream in the freezer." He smiled. "You know what to do. You've done it before."

"Two hours," said Junior. "No way I'm gonna make it."

"When you've finished tidying up the house, give Mannie Katz a call. Meet him somewhere and make sure he gets the envelope."

"What envelope?"

"The one under your plate, Junior." Felix shook his head sadly. "What's the matter with you anyway, you got an astigmatism at your age?"

"Nothing wrong with my eyes," said Junior. He almost added there was nothing wrong with his teeth, either. Bleakly, he stared down at his plate full of congealing food.

Misha could see Junior's feelings were hurt. She waggled her finger at Felix, and rolled her eyes. To cheer Junior up, she gave his arm a squeeze and offered him a piece of raw fish.

"Rude little bastard," said Felix when Junior had left the room.

The flight out wasn't much better. Junior had been given a window seat, the only seat available. Usually the first-class section was almost empty, but now it was full of smiling young men in three-piece suits and smiling young women wearing white blouses and pale blue pleated skirts. Junior snagged a passing stew and asked her what was going on. His fellow passengers were a famous TV evangelist and a mob of singers and writers and dancers and special effects people. "As soon as the bar opens," said Junior, "could I have a double Chivas on the rocks?"

"Quick as I can," said the stew. "I only wish I could join you."

Junior tried on a look of concern. "Something gone wrong, sweetie?"

"A clearance problem. Nothing serious."

"How long we gonna be here?"

"Not long," said the stewardess. She gave him a tired smile. "Would you like a pillow or a magazine?"

"No," said Junior, "I want a drink."

Things hadn't started out well, but they soon got worse. A woman in a plain white blouse and pale blue pleated skirt sat down in the seat next to Junior. Even though the red light wasn't on, she put her seat in the upright position and fastened her safety-belt. Junior looked out of the window. He could see the woman reflected in the glass. She was smiling broadly at the back of his head. There was a JAL 747 parked in the next slip. Junior counted the jet's windows with the same sense of boredom and terror he'd experienced once while counting the holes in an acoustic ceiling tile in his dentist's office.

When he finished counting the windows he counted them again, to make sure he'd got it right the first time. The woman was still watching him, still smiling. He could smell her perfume, feel the heat escaping from her body.

"I've never flown before," she said. "This is my first time."

"Oh yeah?" said Junior. "How interesting."

"A little nervous," said the woman. "But then, who wouldn't be?"

Junior gave her a look he'd learned studying the boa-constrictor at the San Diego zoo.

"Do you believe in God?" said the woman.

"I'll show you what I believe in," said Junior. He flipped open his alligator billfold and waved his Amex platinum in her face. "Easy credit, that's what."

"Money is the root of all evil," said the woman. She spoke in a flat monotone, as if reading from a giant celestial cuecard that nobody else could see.

"That's pure bullshit," said Junior. "It's the lack of money that causes all the problems." He paused for a moment, thinking, and then grinned slyly and said, "How'd you pay for your plane ticket, with a truckload of fucking beets?"

Half an hour later, they were airborne. By the time they'd reached cruising altitude, Junior had put away three quick doubles and had a blood alcohol level of point zero eight and climbing. Better yet, the credits for a Charles Bronson movie were crawling up the little screen tacked to the wall of the head. Junior paged a stew with green eyes and bright red fingernails. He held her hand tightly while he ordered a couple more ounces of Scotch and a pair of headphones. The stew nodded energetically, in a hurry to retrieve her hand.

Junior settled happily back in his seat. Beside him, the thumper was silently reading her bible, rippling heat waves of resentment coming at him every time she turned a page. Not that Junior gave a fuck. Race, creed and colour meant nothing to him. Freedom for all! Let the cream rise to the top! He drank some Scotch, wiped his chin with the back of his hand. Bronson's eyes narrowed. He started blasting away, a big chromed automatic in each hand.

Junior blinked rapidly, trying to focus on the screen.

The sound of the shots reverberated in his head. A girl in the movie screamed prettily. If only the quiche-slinger from Ignacio had been sitting in his lap, everything would have been perfect.

17

Constable Christopher Lambert slipped a button and scratched his chest. The dry cleaner had put too much starch in his shirts again. Peevishly, he adjusted his utility belt to shift the weight of his revolver off his hipbone.

It was two o'clock in the afternoon and eighty-four in the shade. There was no wind. The traffic in both directions was oozing along Georgia Street at a barely perceptible crawl. Lambert yawned. The exhaust fumes were getting to him. He was dying of carbon-monoxide poisoning, heat, and boredom. When a woman in a thin, translucent white summer dress came out of a building and started walking down the sidewalk towards him with the sun backlighting her, he hardly noticed.

"Doesn't she look cool and sweet!" said Constable Paul Furth.

Lambert shrugged. The heat had drained everything out of him. He was exhausted.

"Heat getting to you?" said Furth.

"Was I complaining?"

"You got a rash?"

"Too much starch in my shirt."

They were approaching the intersection of Georgia and Denman. The light turned yellow. Furth tapped the brakes of their Dodge Aspen. A battered Volkswagen van pulled up next to them, in the outside lane. The van needed a new silencer.

Furth concentrated on blocking out the sound. He stared at the traffic light until it turned green, took his foot off the brake pedal and hit the gas. The squad car leapt forward.

The Volkswagen's horn squawked a warning. At the same instant, a low-slung blur of yellow shot in front of the Aspen. Furth stabbed at the brakes with both feet. The nose of the car dipped and Lambert slid across the naugahyde and banged his knee on the metal edge of the computer terminal. The sound of his swearing was drowned out by the screech of rubber on asphalt.

"Fucker ran the light!" said Furth by way of an apology.

Lambert rubbed his knee. He watched the rear end of the yellow Corvette fishtail crazily as the driver struggled to bring the little car under control. Then the Corvette was rocketing down Georgia towards Stanley Park, sprinting for a small gap in the wall of congested traffic that shimmered and glittered in the sunlight half a block away.

Lambert leaned forward and flipped a row of toggle switches, activating the siren and lights. The Corvette bolted, cutting sharply across three lanes to take a right on the one-way road that encircled the thousand acres of the park.

"You know what the difference is between a Corvette and a cactus?" said Lambert.

Furth didn't answer. He was concentrating on his driving.

"The cactus has the prick on the outside," said Lambert.

Furth turned into the park. They sped past the faded brown bulk and sloping roofs of the Royal Vancouver Yacht Club, hundreds of moored sailboats and a gently swaying forest of masts.

A hundred yards in front of them, the Corvette took the zoo turnoff, and pulled into an angled parking slot at the foot of the complex. The driver was still in the car when they caught up with him, the Aspen's siren moaning and shrieking, all the lights spinning and flashing crazily.

Lambert reached over and turned off the siren. He and Furth got out of the squad car and walked over to the Corvette. The driver was leaning back in the seat with his hands behind his head. His face was hidden by big mirrored sunglasses. He had on a pair of mini headphones; a thin wire ran from a tape deck, split into two thinner wires that terminated in small black foam pads stuck in his ears.

Furth pulled the plug. The man's head jerked up, and sunlight flashed off the silver lenses of his glasses.

"Would you please get out of the car, sir," said Lambert.

"Yeah, sure." The man climbed awkwardly out of the Corvette. He smiled and said, "Hi, I'm Larry Snap. Is there a problem?"

"Can I see your driver's licence, please?"

Snap handed Furth his licence. "Black Belt Revolving Records," he said. "The name ring any bells?"

"You ran a red light back there at Denman and Georgia," said Lambert.

"I did?"

"Why do you think we were chasing you?"

"Chasing me?" Larry Snap was amazed. He looked from Furth to Lambert and then back to Furth, as if he suspected a joke and was waiting for the punch line.

"You didn't hear the siren?"

"I had my headphones on. The Sennheiser's. I was listening to a tape."

Furth pulled his ticket book out of his hip pocket.

Larry Snap grimaced anxiously. "I already got a lot of points," he said. "Another bad rap could put me over the edge, cost me my licence."

Furth pushed the button on the end of his ballpoint pen.

"You like a deal on some Springsteen tickets?"

There were five tickets left in Furth's book. It was just enough. He started writing.

Larry Snap waved his arms in the air. "If I can't drive, how in hell am I gonna motivate myself to keep up the payments on my little yellow bird?" he said.

"Have a nice day," said Furth when he had emptied his book.

"And you guys have two nice days each," said Larry Snap. But it was an automatic reaction. They could tell that his heart wasn't in it.

Now that they were in the park, Furth and Lambert had no option but to drive all the way around it. They cruised slowly past Lumberman's Arch and a neglected Parks Board swimming-pool full of sand and débris. From the road there was a sweeping view of the North Shore mountains and much of the inner harbour. Lambert saw a Seabus scoot like a bright orange waterbug out of its berth on the far side of the harbour, and pointed it out to Furth. They drove across the viaduct with its scenic elevated view of Lion's Gate Bridge. It was cool under the canopy of trees, and there was a breeze coming in off the ocean. Lambert looked at his watch. At the rate they were moving along, they'd just make it back to 312 Main in time for end of shift.

They drove slowly past the turn-off to Second Beach, and then left past the fancy restaurant with the glass dome at Ferguson Point.

"You ever eat there?" said Furth.

"Never."

"I hear the food's good but the service is lousy." He paused, thinking. "Or maybe it's the other way around, I forget."

A girl in a yellow bikini ran out of the thin strip of woods that separated the road from the sea wall and the ocean. Lambert was thinking that yellow seemed to be the colour of the day when the girl waved at him. Surprised, he sat up in his seat and waved back. The girl called out, and started running after the car.

Furth pulled over to the side of the road. "Anybody you know?" he said, staring into the rearview mirror.

Lambert twisted in his seat. "Not yet," he said, "but I think I'm already in love."

The girl was breathing heavily by the time she caught up with the car. She was maybe nineteen years old. Her skin was golden brown and she had a light sprinkling of freckles across her nose. Lambert looked deeply into her dark green eyes. What he saw made him immediately realize that whatever she had on her mind, it wasn't romance.

He pushed open his door and started to get out of the Aspen.

18

Eddy Orwell and Judith Lundstrom were sitting side by side on matt black padded stools at the veggie bar at Orwell's gym. Orwell had three tall glasses of lukewarm water lined up in front of him, and one small glass of carrot juice. On the polished wooden counter next to the juice was a paper cup containing his daily intake of vitamin pills. Orwell picked up the cup and shook it gently. The pills made a faint rustling sound. He emptied the cup into the palm of his hand and began eating the pills one by one, washing them down with mouthfuls of water.

Judith sipped her milk, watching him.

Orwell had just finished bench-pressing two tons of iron in increments of 250 pounds. He was pumped up, his blood racing through distended flesh. Judith could see the bulging outline of his muscles through the thick material of his sweatsuit, and she could smell the perfume of his overheated body. He smelled good. He also smelled nervous, worried. It had been more than a month since they'd stopped going out together. Judith had missed Orwell a great deal, but her sense of pride had stopped her from getting in touch with him, despite the temptation.

And now, finally, Orwell had called her.

They were both on their lunch hour. Judith was in her summer uniform – a white blouse and a medium blue A-line skirt, white flats. A dark blue leather purse lay beside her on an empty stool. There was no one else in the veggie bar except the bartender, and he was fifteen feet away, his nose buried in a weightlifting magazine.

Orwell knocked back the last of his pills. His big hand closed over the paper cup, crumpling it. He drank some more water, and swallowed noisily. He'd never been much good at apologies. He felt awkward, and dull. The silence between them started to assume a life of its own, building in intensity.

Judith decided she'd let him stew long enough, that it was

time to get the ball rolling. "I had a weird one this morning," she said.

"Oh yeah?" Orwell gave her his full attention. Being a meter maid was not without its hazards.

"Nice, though."

Orwell frowned. What the hell was that supposed to mean? He drained the third glass of lukewarm water, wiped the gathered sweat from his face with a fleecy grey sleeve.

"It was a Trans Am," said Judith. "A black one, with a sunroof and a tinted windscreen."

"Big eagle on the bonnet, all wings and beak?"

Judith nodded. Like most cops, Eddy knew his cars.

"Meter expired, was it?"

"No, he was parked in front of a fire hydrant."

Orwell frowned. "Can't let 'em get away with a thing like that." There was a celery stick in his glass of carrot juice. He nibbled.

"I was writing the ticket when the guy showed up," said Judith. "Big guy in his late twenties, tall, with a good build. He sat down on the bonnet with his arms folded across his chest, watching me."

"He didn't say anything, just sat there?"

"Showing me his macho hairy chest, all his gold chains. I finished writing the ticket and went to stick it under his windscreen wiper. That's when he made his move, slid off the bonnet and held out his hand. I gave him the ticket. 'You know what I'm going to do with this?' he says. But in a nice tone of voice, sort of kidding around, not mad at all. I shook my head and put my book away. Being careful, letting him know I wasn't going to get involved in an argument."

Judith smiled, remembering.

"He was so quick. In about three seconds he'd folded that ticket up into a cute little dragon with feet and wings and wide open mouth. It had a long twisty tail and everything. You should've seen it, Eddy."

"Just so long as he pays his fine," said Orwell.

"I kind of had a feeling he was the type who wouldn't bother," said Judith. She licked a smear of milk from her upper lip. What happened to a ticket after she'd slapped it on a windscreen was none of her concern. In her business, you had to be a bit of a philosopher.

"What's that called," she said, "folding paper like that?"

"Beats me," said Orwell. He glanced up at the clock over the bar. He was supposed to meet Farley Spears in twenty minutes, and he was probably going to be late. Really late, if Judith was in the mood. He picked up the glass of carrot juice and drank it down, made a face.

"What's the matter?" said Judith.

"Stuff tastes awful."

"What's wrong with it?"

"Nothing. It always tastes awful. It's supposed to, I guess."

"Why do you drink it, then?"

"Because it's good for me."

"Better than eating carrots?"

"You know how many carrots it takes to make a single glass of carrot juice?" Orwell asked.

"No," said Judith. "Do you?"

She looked so sweet, sitting there on the stool with her knees pressed together and her elbows on the counter, leaning towards him, a loose strand of blonde hair falling across her cheek, looking earnest and concerned. Judith spent a lot of money on clothes, but Orwell never found her more attractive than when she was wearing her uniform. He turned towards her, his eyes full of love.

"I can't, Eddy. I have to get back to work."

Orwell started to work up an argument, then decided to let it go. One of the things he liked about Judith was that, like him, she was very conscientious about her job.

"How about dinner?" he said.

"I don't know. You hurt me once, Eddy. I don't want it to happen again."

"It won't. I promise."

"Let me think about it. Call me about six, okay."

"Fine," said Orwell, trying hard not to let his disappointment show.

Judith leaned towards him. She kissed him on his warm, moist, salty cheek, and then slid off her stool and strode towards the door, hips swinging, giving it a little bit extra because she knew he was watching.

At the door, she stopped and turned back to him and said, "Why don't you just come over, Eddy, instead of phoning."

"I could bring a couple of steaks," said Orwell, "and a nice bottle of wine."

Judith shook her head. "No, Eddy. You're taking me out to eat. And it won't be to McDonald's, either."

The door swung shut, leaving Orwell in a celebratory mood. He called out to the bartender, and asked for another glass of carrot juice.

19

Felix Newton, trying to check out the legs of the brunette who was engaged in an apparently futile search for his car, pressed his belly up against the Hertz counter at Seattle International Airport. The girl was easy to look at. She had terrific legs, and looked real chic in her spiffy tailored jacket with the company logo over the breast pocket. But Felix was close to losing patience with her anyway. The beige four-door Caprice he'd reserved at the Hertz counter at LAX was lost somewhere deep in the electronic bowels of the Hertz computer. He'd been waiting for the car to pop up on the screen for ten minutes now, and he was still feeling nauseous from his flight; all that altitude and the cheapo cold plate they'd served for lunch.

Felix glanced around the terminal. He'd told Junior not to bother coming out to meet him, but had hoped that the kid might show up all the same. Fat chance. He was all alone, and likely to stay that way until Misha got back from the carousel, where she was waiting for her matched set of six pigskin suitcases to drop down the chute. Felix had given her the suitcases for her last birthday. It had been a big mistake. The fucking things were beautiful to look at, but they were also bulky as hell and weighed a ton. Naturally, since then, Misha had never gone anywhere without them.

"I can't get you a beige Caprice," said the brunette, "but we've got a red one all gassed up and ready to go." She was wearing a name tag, a small rectangle of black plastic with white letters. But she'd pinned the tag on upside down, and so far Felix hadn't been able to get a good look at it. She smiled at him. "Would red be okay, Mr Newton?"

"I'm sorry," said Felix. "The car has to be beige or brown or maybe dark blue. No bright colours, isn't that what I said?"

Still smiling, the girl turned away from him and resumed her attack on the keys of the computer terminal.

Felix sighed. He used the edge of his credit card to play a

tune called impatience on the Formica countertop. His mind drifted. He wondered what kind of job Junior had done of cleaning up his British Properties rancher. A lousy one, probably. Felix looked at his watch, at the liver spots on the back of his hand. All the spots were similar, but no two were identical. There were lots of them, though. He brought the credit card down a little more vigorously on the counter. The girl jabbed at her keyboard.

Seen from a certain angle, she seemed remarkably familiar. He guessed she was in her early thirties. If he'd ever used her, it would have been a dozen or more years ago. And in a bit part, not a major role or he'd remember her name. Despite his advancing age, he had a memory like a whole fucking herd of elephants.

But there was something about the line of her neck, the angle of her jaw . . .

Only one way to find out. Felix stepped back from the counter. He broke into a little sideways shuffle, threw his arms wide and burst into song.

Would you like to be an actress
Would you care to be a star
People everywhere would know you
No matter who and where you are
You only live once, my sweet
Why settle for the role of "fan"
When it's so much nicer to be
A leading lady in
The arms of a leading maaaaaan!

"What a wonderful voice you have," said the girl. The big kiss-off. Felix's feet stopped moving. He let his arms fall to his sides. What was he, auditioning?

"Your name tag's upside down," he said.

The girl got up from the computer terminal and came over to the counter. She unclipped the black plastic rectangle, refastened it. Her name was Shirley. "How about a cream-coloured Ford," she said.

"I wish my secretary was here," said Felix. "She's really

much better at making these decisions than I am. Is it a four-door model?"

Shirley nodded. "Would you like to take a look at it?"

"Is the ashtray clean?"

"Absolutely spotless."

"If it isn't, do I get a complimentary ballpoint pen or some glassware or something?"

"I can give you a complimentary pen right now, if you like."

"You're conceding the ashtray's going to be dirty?"

"No, Mr Newton. All I'm saying is that if you want a free pen, I'd be happy to give you one."

"You mean, if that's what it takes to get me to accept the wrong colour car."

Shirley gave him yet another smile.

"I do a lot of business with Hertz," said Felix. "This is the first time anything's gone wrong. I've been recommending you to my friends for years, and now this. What am I gonna tell them, huh?"

"Tell them you talked us out of a valuable free pen," said Shirley. She slapped a standard contract form down on the counter, starting writing. "How much insurance would you like?"

"The max," said Felix. "I like to live right on the edge, so why not be prepared for the worst?"

Felix could see Shirley thought he was a kidder, kind of dumb, just another old fart in the wind. Suddenly he was exhausted. The song and dance had taken a lot out of him, more than he'd realized. Misha was a crummy driver but he was going to let her handle the Ford. The way he felt now, three hours on the turnpike could kill him. And anyway, he needed his rest. There was a lot to do in Vancouver. This guy Mannie Katz seemed to have gone to sleep on him.

Felix signed the Hertz rental form, and stuck Shirley's pen in his pocket. It looked good there, the chrome clip gleaming brightly against the dark blue cloth of his conservatively-cut suit jacket. He held out his hand for the keys, and when Shirley handed them to him, managed to give the tips of her fingers a friendly little squeeze.

20

A gust of summer wind had finally blown Mannie Katz's rayon shirt and bile-green twenty-dollar suit out of the fork of the tree he'd tossed them into on the night of the murder.

Furth's radio call had been responded to by a second squad car, two unmarked vehicles, the crime lab van, and Homer Bradley's bone-white Chrysler Cordoba. Bradley soon had half a dozen uniformed men thrashing through the shrubbery. They were looking for evidence, but all they'd come up with so far was a few empty beer bottles and an old candy-bar wrapper.

Bradley talked to the girl in the yellow bikini while his two homicide detectives, Willows and Parker, watched Mel Dutton take dozens of photographs of the crime scene. Over the years, Dutton had developed a certain style. While he worked, he never stopped moving. The power winder of his Nikon whirred and clicked ceaselessly as he circled the dark and crumpled pile of blood-stained clothing. Every time he took a picture it was from a slightly different angle. The white glare of his flash probed into all the folds and creases of the cheap suit, the thin white shirt, the unbelievably loud tie.

A pair of steel-rimmed glasses lay half out of the breast pocket of the suitcoat. The lenses briefly reflected a matched pair of miniature Mel Duttons; then he triggered his flash unit and the crouching, distorted images were wiped away in a sudden burst of light.

When he was satisfied that he had enough shots of the clothing, Dutton stepped back several paces and switched to a 135mm telephoto lens. He arched his back and began to photograph Mannie's undersized shoes, which were still dangling by the laces from a branch about thirty feet up.

"We're going to have to bring in a hook-and-ladder," said Willows.

Parker nodded in agreement. She'd watched Chris Lambert

try to shinny up the trunk, slide back down and ruin his pants. "You want me to make a call?"

"Not just yet. We might as well wait until Goldstein finishes up."

Jerry Goldstein was from forensics. He was the department's whizz kid, a tall thin man with curly blond hair and oversized horn-rimmed glasses that kept sliding down his nose. Goldstein had been standing diffidently off to the side, staying out of the way while Dutton did his job. Now that Dutton was through, he knelt to open a battered aluminium suitcase, and removed his fingerprint kit. He dusted the glasses first. They were clean. He put them in a plastic ziplock evidence bag, and tucked the bag away in a corner of his suitcase. The buttons on the suit were plastic. Goldstein dusted them down one by one. He picked up several partials. Experience had taught him that none of the prints would stand up in court, even as corroborative evidence. But he saved them anyway, because experience had also taught him that when it came to corroborative evidence, you could never be sure what would be accepted in court.

Crouching, Goldstein used the tip of his Bic pen to explore the stiff folds of the suit. Dried blood flaked away like patches of rust. He went through the pockets, and found a quantity of lint, two dimes, an American quarter, a partial roll of breath mints, and a hundred-dollar bill that was saturated with dried blood. He dropped the lint and coins and mints into several evidence bags, and waved the bill at Willows and Parker.

"Got something for us, Jerry?" said Willows.

"Take a look at this," said Goldstein.

In the few small areas of the bill that had not been soaked with blood, the paper was crisp and new. Willows could faintly see many criss-crossed lines, thin scars, indentations where the bill had been folded over and over again.

"A hundred's a hell of a lot to pay a street hooker," said Goldstein. "But it'd make real good bait."

Mel Dutton had wandered over. "Depends what you're paying for," he said. Parker smiled at him, and he hastily added, "That's what I hear from my pals in vice, anyway."

"What I'd like to know," said Willows, "is why the killer walked away from a hundred-dollar bill?"

"And forty-five cents and most of a package of Certs," added Goldstein facetiously. The girl in the bikini was watching him, and he'd felt he had to say something. He smiled at her, and she looked away.

"You through yet?" said Bradley, peering over the girl's shoulder.

"That's all for now," Goldstein replied. The field was of interest only because it was where the bits and pieces of the puzzle were collected. It was the lab work that fascinated him, because that was where the pieces were fitted together, and the puzzle was solved. He put the hundred-dollar bill in yet another evidence bag, locked up his gleaming suitcase. The girl was watching him again.

"Whatever you find," said Willows quietly, "I'd appreciate it if you called me first."

"Sure," said Goldstein. "No problem."

Bradley had finished with the girl in the bikini. He caught Willows' eye, and motioned him down the slope, in the direction of the beach. Willows nodded. "I'll meet you back at the car," he said to Parker.

"What's he want?"

"I don't have any idea. If I find out, I'll let you know."

Willows followed his superior through the trees, the soles of his shoes slipping on the treacherous carpet of dead fir needles. By the time he came out of the trees, Bradley had crossed the narrow strip of asphalt that circled the park, and was lowering himself on to the sun-warmed granite of the sea wall. The six-mile long wall of stone had been built by a parks board employee named James Cunningham. There was an annual footrace around the park to commemorate his achievement. Willows knew about the race because his wife had run it, as had both his children.

Bradley took out a cigar, and lit it. He glanced up at Willows, who was standing next to him, and then turned to contemplate the beach.

"Beautiful day, isn't it?"

"So far," said Willows.

Bradley chuckled appreciatively, exhaling a cloud of smoke.

The bows of the freighters in the outer harbour were pointed towards the beach, which meant an outgoing tide was dragging at their anchors. Willows wondered what it was like, being a seaman. His attention was diverted by three small boys who were kicking a brightly coloured ball along the shoreline.

"Tell me what you think," said Bradley. He patted the block of granite beside him. "Sit down, Jack. Make yourself comfy."

Willows moved a few feet upwind of the cigar smoke, and sat down on a stone. His legs dangled over the edge. At this part of the park, there was a wide expanse of sand between the ocean and the sea wall. There was no danger of erosion from winter storms, and so the wall was only a few feet high. One of the boys was running down the beach with the ball in his arms, closely pursued by his two friends.

"The killer must have *planned* to steal the Econoline van," said Willows. "Otherwise, he wouldn't have been carrying the alligator clips he used to hot-wire the damn thing."

"So what does that tell us?"

"It was premeditated murder. Murder in the first degree. Twenty-five years when we catch him. No chance of parole." Willows drummed his heels against the granite wall. "I think he killed the kid, dumped the van, walked right past where those three kids are playing, and went for a swim."

"A backstroke getaway. In the nude." Bradley grinned. "I like it, Jack. You got the film rights all wrapped up?"

"I think we can assume he had a bathing suit on under his suit. You notice his clothes, Homer?"

Bradley spat a shred of tobacco out of his mouth. "I was busy with the bikini. What about them?"

"They were cheap, outdated, disposable. All he had to do was walk into the ocean, wash off the blood, swim a few hundred yards along the shoreline, and walk out. Who'd pay any attention, even if someone did happen to see him?"

"After he takes his dip, then what?"

"He's got another set of clothes waiting somewhere along the beach, or in a parked car. He towels himself off, changes, drives away."

"Roll credits?"

"We're supposed to catch him first, Inspector."

"Oh yeah, right."

Bradley heard the hiss of roller-skates on asphalt. He looked up just as a black girl in a red and white striped bathing suit

110

shot past him. The girl was skinny as a barber's pole, and had her hair arranged in stiff braids that stuck out from her forehead like antennae. Bradley couldn't help smiling. Much to his surprise, she glanced over her shoulder and smiled back at him, gave him the sweetest smile he'd seen in years. He was so stunned he almost dropped his cigar.

"Parker and I went down to the morgue and examined the body," said Willows. "There were seventy-odd puncture wounds, Inspector. The killer slashed himself into a frenzy, and it just doesn't make sense."

"Why not?"

"Because up to a point, the killer seems to have planned everything very carefully, been very cool. Then it breaks down. Why buy those magazines so close to where he picked up the kid? Why steal a fifty-cent roll of breath mints when he could afford to buy them? We got a very good description of him from that Chinese woman. Why did he take the risk?"

"Guys like him take risks all the time. It's what they get off on."

Willows reached down and pulled off one of his brogues. He wriggled his toes. It felt good. He noticed that his shoe was scuffed, and that the heel was badly worn. It occurred to him that he was starting to let himself slide, that there must be other signs of his descent. "There's something else," he said to Bradley.

Bradley's cigar had gone out. The match made a brittle sound as he dragged it across the granite. He exhaled with pleasure and said, "What's that, Jack?"

"The guy who killed the kid almost certainly murdered that girl I found in the creek up past Squamish," said Willows.

Bradley gaped at him. The smile from the girl on the roller-skates, and now this. The day was full of surprises.

Willows told Bradley about the vending-machine photograph he and Rossiter had found in Naomi Lister's white shorts, and how the shorts had also been left in the fork of a tree. He told him about the blue Smurf tattooed on her arm, and about the wedge of flesh that had been cut out of the arm of the boy in the morgue, the trace of blue at the perimeter of the wound. Bradley listened carefully, not saying a word. His cigar went out again, unnoticed. When Willows had finished, Bradley

111

immediately said, "I want you to call Squamish. Get the Mounties to wire down her picture and anything else they've got."

"I've already done it," said Willows. "It should be on your desk by now."

"We've got to get moving on this," said Bradley. The words rang hollow, as they invariably did. He frowned at the harbour, as if the view displeased him.

Willows took his other shoe off, and both his socks. He stuffed the socks into the shoes and rolled up his trousers, let himself drop from the sea wall to the beach. The sand was very hot. "We're looking for a short, paunchy bald guy who walked out of the ocean somewhere between here and English Bay, sometime between sunset and eleven o'clock, which was when Parker made her call. Roughly a two-hour time-span on a warm night in the middle of August. What would you say our chances are, Inspector?"

"Maybe Goldstein'll come up with something."

Willows bent and picked up a shard of glass that had been half-buried beneath the sand. "You see the weapon?"

"What about it?"

"Maybe you could put Farley Spears on it for me, see if he can track it down."

"Yeah, sure. Anything else?"

"Naomi Lister's father said she'd been living here in the city for the past year or so. Parker and I are going to try to make contact with some of her friends."

"Fine," said Bradley.

"We thought we'd concentrate on that angle of the case pretty much to the exclusion of everything else," said Willows carefully.

"Sounds good to me, Jack."

Willows picked another piece of glass out of the hot, dusty sand. He saw now that the pieces were from a Coke bottle. In the distance, the three boys were chasing the brightly-coloured ball back up the beach towards him. Their voices were high-pitched, unformed. As they drew nearer, Willows noticed that the oldest of the three was about the same age as his son. The boy had that same lithe, hard body, the ungainly grace of movement. His hair was brown, too, although a little darker than Sean's. Willows idly wondered what colour the boy's eyes were. Sean's were dark blue, like Sheila's. Brown was dominant, of course, and since the separation, Willows had come to resent that minor genetic quirk. Unreasonably, he wished their child had looked a little more like his father.

He clinked the two broken pieces of glass together, moved them around to see if he could make them fit.

There was entirely too much vandalism nowadays. The bottles were worth a dime each at any corner store, but even if they were worth a dollar, it probably wouldn't make any difference. A beach full of broken glass. Just another symptom. The world his son would inherit was changing fast, and not for the better.

21

Something over there to his left. Crouched down low. Staying in the shadows, circling slowly around behind him.

Mannie rolled over on his side. Evasive action. He fell off the chesterfield, out of his dream. His eyes popped open. He sat up, stunned, breathing heavily through his open mouth.

The sound of the telephone filled the house.

He looked at his watch. It was two o'clock in the morning. On the coffee table in front of him an empty wine bottle and a cardboard bucket full of chicken bones and congealing fat sat at eye-level. He blinked. There was an old black and white movie on the TV, but no sound. He burped and scratched his stomach. Except for his jockey shorts and his socks, he was naked. The telephone kept ringing. He pushed himself to his feet and went to answer it.

"You sleep all day and all night too?" said Junior.

Junior sounded like he was in a jovial mood. His voice was light, teasing. There was a soft percussive throbbing in the background, and then the lonely and desolate big-mosquito whine of a steel guitar. Mannie couldn't make out the lyrics, but he had a feeling he wasn't missing much. If Junior liked it, he doubted that he would.

"Hello?" said Junior in that tickling voice. "Is anybody at home?"

"Be right back," Mannie said, and put down the phone without waiting for an answer. Moving very fast, he went down the darkened hallway to his bedroom, edged carefully over to the window until he had a view of the street. Junior's black Trans Am was parked right in front of the house. The brake lights pulsed rhythmically; bright smears of red that stained the asphalt and the cars of Mannie's neighbours. It took him a few seconds to figure out that Junior was hitting his pedal in time to the music playing on his radio. He stared out the window at the sleek bulk of the car, waxed paint glistening in the incandescent glow of the streetlight at the end of the block, chrome winking at him as if hoping to share an obscure joke. There was no movement that he could see inside the car, although with the tinted windows he couldn't see much. The brakes kept flashing, little explosions of red that flared and faded and flared again. Mannie had the eerie and somewhat dislocating feeling that the Trans Am was a living, breathing thing; a creature of the night that was capable of swallowing him whole and spitting out his bones.

Junior revved the big V-8 engine. The sash window vibrated in its wooden frame. Mannie felt the cold glass shiver against the tip of his nose. He hurried back to the telephone. He was wide awake now, and even more frightened than he had been in his dream. "I'm back," he said into the receiver. Fear made him aggressive. "What the hell you want at this time of night?"

"A cup of hot chocolate and a bran muffin," said Junior mildly. "You know this town better'n anybody else I can think of, you've lived here your whole life, right? So come on out and show me around."

"It's two o'clock in the fucking morning!"

"So what d'you want me to do, synchronize my watch?"

Mannie slipped his hand under his jockeys and used his fingers to comb the pubic hair at the root of his penis. He was still trying to think of something witty to say when Junior added, "Also, I got an urgent message for you. From Felix."

"Gimme a couple of minutes to get dressed."

"And to brush your teeth," said Junior.

Mannie hung up, but the music kept getting louder. Junior must've turned up his radio, or tape deck or whatever it was he was listening to. The band sounded like it was right outside Mannie's bedroom window, playing its heart out and waiting for the flower pots to start dropping.

Mannie's clothes were scattered around the living-room. He turned off the TV and got dressed. If his breath smelled like anything, it was the Colonel's chicken. What was wrong with that?

They went to Bino's. Mannie hadn't ordered a cup of cocoa since he was a kid, but he'd seen the bran muffins and figured they had to be the biggest muffins in town.

"This is one huge mother of a muffin," said Junior to the waitress. He leaned out into the aisle, gripping the edge of the table to keep his balance, and stared down at her legs. "I like your ankles, too," he said. The waitress smiled and moved off. Junior picked up a knife and cut his muffin in half. The muffin was so hot it was steaming. Junior dug whipped butter out of a little paper cup, spread the butter on the muffin.

"My mother used to say that if a girl had slim ankles, you could be sure she had a good figure. What she didn't tell me is that there are a lot more interesting ways to find out how a woman is built. You know what I mean?"

"Sure," said Mannie. He sipped at his glass of two per cent milk. The milk was so cold it made the roof of his mouth ache. He swallowed.

"Feelies," said Junior. "One hand under the angora, the other up her skirt. Like the sailor said to his sweetheart, 'All hands on deck!'"

Junior ripped open a plastic container of raspberry jam. He tried to spread the jam on the muffin. The muffin crumbled and fell apart. He applied the jam haphazardly, in runny gobs.

Mannie took another sip of milk. With his left hand he reached below the table to gently touch the haft of his Italian switchblade. When he looked up, Junior was watching him. Junior's strong jaws rose and fell as he demolished a chunk of muffin. He grinned at Mannie.

"The girl you've been looking for, Carly?"

"What about her?"

"She's living somewhere out in the suburbs, with a guy named Walter."

"I don't know any Walters," said Mannie.

"Neither do I." Junior pointed at Mannie's glass of milk. "You gonna drink that, or what?"

"It's too cold. I'm waiting for it to warm up."

"Why didn't you order a glass of warm milk in the first place?"

"You got an address for me?"

"I love a self-starter," said Junior. He licked a crumb from his upper lip, reached into his breast pocket and handed Mannie a sealed buff envelope that smelled strongly of cologne.

Mannie wedged his thumbnail under the flap. Junior held out

his hand. "Not here, please. Use the can so I can say no when Felix asks me was I there when you looked inside." Junior gave Mannie a wink. "Felix is happiest when I keep a certain distance," he explained.

Mannie nodded slowly. He thought about the risks involved in going into the washroom, decided that there weren't any because if Junior had something in mind for him, there were easier ways.

"I'll be back in a minute."

Junior waved a jam-smeared knife at him. "Take your time, enjoy the moment."

Mannie went into a cubicle and pulled the flush. He tore open the envelope. There was a single sheet of white bond paper inside, a typed invitation to Sunday Brunch at Felix Newton's rancher up in the Properties. Instructions to dress for white wine. Whatever the hell that meant. There was no address. Mannie had no idea where the house was, and doubted it was listed in the phone book. He'd have to ask Junior, he supposed. He crumpled up the envelope and piece of paper, threw them into the toilet. Got everything down the tubes with his third flush.

When he got back to the table his glass of milk had vanished, and so had Junior. He'd left the bill, though. Mannie paid the waitress with the nice ankles. He was careful not to overtip. He had just enough money on him for the cab fare home.

117

22

Jerry Goldstein's office was a dusty, lidless glass box at the far end of the crime lab; his desk a paper-cluttered slab of steel painted vaguely to resemble oak veneer. Goldstein sat behind the desk in a captain's chair, comfortably perched on a fat crocheted cushion. The chair was on castors. It squeaked minutely as he leant forward to thumb slowly through a stack of pink message slips wedged under the dial of his telephone. He glanced up as Willows and Parker came in, smiled at Parker and said, "Be with you in just a sec."

Willows glanced at his watch. He'd had lunch a little under half an hour ago. A glass of milk and a tuna melt, coleslaw on the side. Something had been off, and he suspected the tuna. He rubbed his stomach and sat down in a folding metal chair painted bright orange. To match Goldstein's hair, maybe.

Parker wandered over to the bookshelf behind Goldstein's desk. There was a jar of cloudy formaldehyde on the top shelf. She peered at the label affixed to the lid of the jar, but the words were illegible, so badly faded that they were hardly there at all. She picked up the jar and held it tilted against the glare of the overhead fluorescents, turned it this way and that. A pale, shiny grey lump pressed against the glass, drifted away. Something that looked like a cauliflower, or a bunch of mushrooms growing shoulder to shoulder out of a single stalk. Parker rotated the jar, trying for a better angle, another glimpse.

Goldstein shuffled through the pile of pink slips, rearranging them in order of urgency. As usual, he looked as if he'd just stepped off the front cover of a fashion magazine. Today he was wearing a light grey houndstooth jacket with narrow lapels and patch pockets, charcoal slacks, a crisp white button-down oxford cloth shirt and a shiny black leather tie. The collar buttons of the shirt were unfastened. The tie was loose. The overall effect was to give Goldstein a casual elegance. Or so he hoped. Within the department, he was famous for his collection of leather ties, which he owned in all widths and colours. He wore the ties in the mistaken belief that they gave him an added dimension, hinted that behind the crisp white shirts and scholarly tortoise-shell glasses there resided a wide-open mind, perhaps even a slightly kinky temperament. He brought the heel of his hand down hard, driving a staple through the stack of pink messages. The desk vented a metallic echo. He looked over at Parker, who was still squinting into the murky depths of the jar.

"Never seen a human brain before?"

Parker put the jar carefully back down on the shelf. Motes of disturbed dust danced in the light.

"Where do you want to start?" Goldstein said to Jack Willows.

"With the weapon."

There was a rectangular cardboard box on Goldstein's desk. The box had originally contained a pair of Hart penny loafers. Goldstein removed the lid and flipped the box upside down, dumping the contents across the ersatz oak. He gingerly tested the edge of the knife against the ball of his thumb. There were several small nicks and a filigree of crusted blood in the curve of the blade, where steel had forcibly met bone. The blood type was A Positive, and the blood had come from the boy in the morgue. Goldstein flipped the knife in the air and caught it neatly. The weapon felt comfortable in his hand; it had a nice weight and balance. He glanced at Willows, sensed a growing impatience.

"Unusual design, Jack. Never seen one like it before. Not much good for stabbing or slashing. Odd choice for a killer. But obviously a tool of some kind, wouldn't you say?"

"Yeah, right." Obviously.

"But what kind of a tool?" said Goldstein. It wasn't a rhetorical question. He fiddled with the knot of his tie, waiting for an answer.

Willows turned to Parker. "You want to hold him while I pour that jar of brains down his throat, or shall I hold him while you pour?"

"You hold him," said Parker.

"It's a tool for cutting lead," said Goldstein quickly.

119

"Cutting lead?" said Parker.

Goldstein nodded. "The lead strips in stained glass windows."

"Where can I get one?"

"Almost anywhere." Goldstein turned to Willows. "There are several dozen suppliers in the metropolitan area. Or you can order one by mail through any of the handicraft magazines." Goldstein sighted along the flat of the blade at his pile of pink slips. "A very popular item, this knife. You want to work with stained glass, you've got to have one."

"Where's it made?" said Parker.

"West Germany. Carbon steel, very high quality. Cost you about thirty dollars, if you're looking for a hobby."

"I'll stick with my train set."

"Anything else?" said Willows.

"On the knife? Zilch."

Willows had taken out his notebook and a matt-black Uniball pen. He turned a fresh page and wrote briefly, using his own peculiar brand of shorthand, his writing disciplined and concise. "What about the stuff that dropped out of the tree?"

Goldstein shrugged disdainfully. "The guy didn't spend a lot of money on his wardrobe, that's for sure." He grinned, showing large white teeth. "In fact, his clothes were so cheap they didn't even have labels."

"Dry cleaning marks?"

"The quality we're talking about, when it gets dirty you throw it away."

"Well then, Jerry, what *do* you have for me?"

"The shoes were sevens. The shirt was a thirty-three sleeve sixteen neck. The trousers had a thirty-six inch waistband, twenty-six inch leg. I look into my crystal ball and see a man who is short and stout."

Willows was making notes again, his head bowed over the page.

"Then I stop peering into the crystal ball," said Goldstein. "And I take a look *inside* the shoes."

Willows stopped writing. He glanced up.

"Know what I find?"

"What?"

"Stains. From blisters that had burst."

120

"He was wearing shoes that were too small for him, is that what you're saying?"

"It's a possibility."

"The old woman in the grocery store," said Parker, "she told us he walked with a limp."

Willows nodded, remembering.

"And the clothes in the park, we found everything but socks."

"You can figure out the blood type from the blister, can't you, Jerry?" said Willows.

"We're working on it."

"Soon?"

"We should have the results some time this afternoon, hopefully." Goldstein leant back in his chair. The castors squeaked. He locked his fingers behind his head and looked up at the ceiling. The round lenses of his glasses reflected light from the fixtures. It was impossible to tell whether his eyes were open or closed. "Fingerprints," he said. "You already know about the partials on the suitcoat buttons. We found more on the Certs package and on a couple of loose coins in the trouser pockets. Nothing worth running through the computer, though. And almost certainly nothing that would stand up in court."

"What about the magazines, the cigar tube?"

"On the tube we found most of an index finger and a thumb. I'm just guessing, in an educated sort of way, but I'd say that if you ever matched them up, you'd find that you'd collared the clerk who sold the cigar."

"Did you find out what brand it is?" said Parker.

"What, the cigar?"

Parker nodded.

"One thing for sure." Goldstein smiled. "It wasn't an El Producto."

"Pardon me?" said Parker.

"Why bother, is what I'm saying." Goldstein turned to Willows, who nodded his head in agreement. Both men sensed what the less experienced Parker did not – that the cigar was a dead end.

"What about the blue mark on the victim's arm, at the edge of the wound?" said Willows.

"You were right, it was tattooist's ink. I phoned Squamish. The pathologist is sending down a tissue sample from that girl you found in the river."

"Naomi Lister." Willows moved on. "Was all the blood in the Econoline van A Positive?"

"Every last gallon of it."

"What else did you get out of the van?"

"Some loose hairs that don't match the victim's. Otherwise, nothing. The vehicle was spotless. Washed and waxed, you might say."

"The connecting wires under the dash, you get anywhere with that?"

"Not really, Jack. The soldering was pretty sloppy; a home-made job. The wire and alligator clips you can buy pretty well anywhere they sell wire and clips."

Willows made a few notes. "I guess that's about it, except for the hundred-dollar bill. Nobody throws away a hundred dollars, so I think it's safe to assume the money was left behind by accident, in the heat of the moment." Willows was struck by a sudden thought. "The bill *is* genuine, isn't it?"

"As real as money can be. And your next question is, why all the folds and creases in a brand-new bill, am I correct?"

"So far, Jerry."

"Mel Dutton took some great snaps. Black and white. Fine grain, terrific resolution. They're circulating. Who knows, maybe we'll get lucky."

"That's just great, Jerry."

Goldstein shrugged. "All I know for sure about money is that I never seem to have enough of it."

"You got a set of Dutton's pictures for us?" said Willows.

"Two sets," amended Parker.

Goldstein used a sideways flip of his wrist to skim an eight-by-ten envelope across the room.

Willows unwound the thin red string that sealed the envelope. He pulled out a handful of glossies. The photographed hundred-dollar bill looked like a reverse image in minute scale of the street grid of a perfectly rectangular city: a confusing network of intersecting white lines on a background of grey. Robert Borden's heavy face had been aged a thousand years by the dense hatchwork. The bill was hardly recognizable.

"I like a puzzle," said Goldstein. "Since I had a couple of dollar bills in my wallet, I thought, hey, why not give it a try. In about two minutes I had a five-aspirin headache and in about three minutes I'd stopped caring if you ever found the guy."

"Where's the original?" said Parker.

Goldstein fished in his pocket for a key, unlocked the top drawer of his desk. He pulled out a plastic evidence bag. Tiny flakes of dried blood had collected in the bottom left corner. Goldstein shook the bag and the flakes drifted upwards, like black snow.

Willows went over to the desk and held out his hand. Goldstein looked at the hand as if it had six fingers. After a moment he gave the bag to Willows.

"I signed that money out, Jack. That makes me responsible for it."

Willows smiled. "Tough shit, Jerry, because I'm going to take the whole squad over to McDonald's for lunch." He slipped the envelope in his breast pocket and started towards the door.

"I almost forgot," said Goldstein to Parker. "Next Sunday's the fourth annual Tatlow Park Invitational Croquet Tournament. Would you like to come?"

Parker hesitated.

"Nice crowd," said Goldstein. "Lots of singles. All you have to do is wear whites and bring along a couple of bottles of decent wine. The food's taken care of. Cold cuts, stuff like that."

"What time Sunday?" said Parker.

"We kick off at two o'clock sharp."

"Are you going to wear a white leather tie?"

"Probably," said Goldstein.

"You actually own one, do you?"

"Yeah, sure."

Parker pointed. "That one's naugahyde, right?"

"What?" Goldstein frowned. "You think I'm the kind of guy who'd wear a naugahyde tie?"

"Definitely," said Parker.

23

The telephone rang.

Willows blinked, and the hundred-dollar bill lying on his desk suddenly came back into focus. He sat up a little straighter in his chair. Stifling a yawn, he picked up the phone. It was Pat Rossiter, calling him from Squamish.

"What's all this about a tattoo, Jack?"

Willows collected his thoughts. He told Rossiter about the wedge-shaped slice of flesh carved out of the dead boy's forearm, in the exact same spot where Naomi Lister's tattoo had been located.

"And you're looking for what?" It might have been the connection, but Rossiter didn't sound particularly interested.

"I think the boy had an identical tattoo to Naomi Lister's, and that it was cut out of his arm to eliminate any connection between the two of them."

"Wait a minute. What about that picture we found in the girl's shorts? If you're right, why didn't the killer grab the snapshot, instead of leaving it behind?"

"He made a mistake."

"I don't think so, Jack. The coroner's report was filed this morning. Death by misadventure. No blame attached." Rossiter paused, but Willows had nothing to say. "The water in her lungs came from the creek, not Alfred Hitchcock's bathtub. The various bruises and abrasions on her body were entirely consistent with the kind of beating she'd have taken drifting down that creek. And there's more. You listening?"

"Yeah, sure." Willows was beginning to feel a trifle irritated, but he kept his voice flat and calm.

"The pathologist's report noted a blood carbon-monoxide level of fifteen point eight per cent." A distant match flared. Willows heard Rossiter inhale deeply, the rustling of paper as he turned a page. "You know as well as I do," the Mountie continued, "that major among the symptoms of carbon-monoxide poisoning is a marked tendency towards impaired judgement. Naomi Lister could easily have put herself at extreme risk without being aware of what she was doing."

Willows thought back, recalled in his mind the overgrown logging road, the smears of oil and globules of fresh grease on the grass, the torn earth and tread marks of a four-wheel drive vehicle. It'd be easy to damage an exhaust system going up that mountain. And that would account for the carbon-monoxide poisoning, no doubt about it.

"What I want to know," said Willows, "is who drove her up that mountain, and where was he when she decided to go for a swim?"

Rossiter sighed into the receiver. "Probably off in the woods somewhere. Smoking a joint, drinking a beer. Maybe taking a nap under a tree."

"Were there any residual traces of alcohol or other drugs in the body?"

"Negative."

"Indications that she'd recently had sex?"

"No, nothing like that."

"So what's her mystery companion so worried about? Is skinny-dipping with a juvie such a big deal up there in the woods?"

"Maybe he's a married man."

"Or a multiple murderer."

"Let's hope not," said Rossiter. But his tone of voice made it clear he wasn't too worried about the possibility. Belatedly, Willows realized that Rossiter had not phoned to enquire about his request for a tissue sample, but simply to inform him that the Squamish detachment of the RCMP had closed Naomi Lister's file.

Willows thanked Rossiter for his help, brusquely cut off his attempt to make small talk, and hung up. Flipping open his notebook, he methodically recorded the gist of their brief conversation. The fact that Naomi Lister's blood had contained high levels of carbon monoxide nagged at him. He pushed the problem to the back of his mind. Let his subconscious worry about it: he didn't have the time.

Claire Parker strolled into the squad room. She went over to the water cooler and pointed at it, gave Willows an enquiring look. He shook his head. When she'd finished drinking, Parker shook the last few drops of water from the conical paper cup and then balanced the cup upside down on her head.

Willows had needed a lift. He smiled, and Parker curtsied in acknowledgement. Willows locked the hundred-dollar bill away in the bottom drawer of his desk.

It was time to hit the bricks.

24

Mannie lived on East 30th, in the shadow of Queen Elizabeth Park. His faded shingle house was only half a block from Nat Bailey Stadium, home of the Canadians, a Triple-A franchise affiliated with the Milwaukee Brewers. When there was a game, Mannie could hear the crowd noises in his kitchen even with the window shut.

Junior drove past the empty stadium and turned left, cruised down 30th at a steady five miles an hour, the dual exhausts of the black Trans Am burbling softly in his wake. It was Sunday morning, half past ten. Junior was early. With any luck he'd catch Mannie in his Pooh Bear jammies.

The street in front of the house was empty. No cars, no kids, nothing. Junior tapped the brakes, slowed almost to a stop and turned sharply right. The car shuddered as the front wheels hit the curb. Junior nosed up on the sidewalk and pushed slowly through the flimsy picket fence. Wood snapped and splintered. A board popped loose and cartwheeled into a neighbour's yard.

Junior stomped on the gas.

The big V-8 howled. The fat-track Goodyear Eagle GT's tore up the grass, spat out clods of earth, sprayed pebbles and small stones across the road. Junior smelled burnt rubber. Then the Positraction kicked in and the car bolted, the acceleration throwing him back against the seat. He stabbed at the brake pedal and the car immediately began to drift sideways, the rear end creeping around on him. Spinning the wheel, using both hands, he just managed to get straightened out before he smacked into the side of the house.

The Trans Am stopped dead. Junior's knee hit the underside of the steering-column hard enough to make his eyes water. The engine stalled. Cursing, he went for the Colt Magnum in the glove compartment, thought better of it, slumped over the steering-wheel and closed his eyes.

Mannie came out on his postage-stamp of a front porch in

his red imitation silk dressing-gown, a bowl of Rice Crispies in his left hand. He saw the black Trans Am squatting malevolently in his yard, the gaping hole in his fence, his ruined lawn and the dent in the house his father had built and lived in all his life.

Dropping the bowl of cereal, Mannie stormed down the steps and across the lawn, yanked on Junior's door and shredded a fingernail.

Junior opened his eyes one at a time. He squinted lazily out at Mannie through the tinted glass, and then reached out and hit a chrome button. The window powered down.

Mannie struck his head inside the car and said, "What the fuck are you doing to my house?"

"Knock, knock," said Junior.

"You stupid shit!"

Junior patted the passenger seat. "Hop in. It's time for brunch."

Mannie sucked at his injured finger. He tasted blood, warm and salty. "How come you're so early?" he said.

"Get in," said Junior. He turned the ignition key. The engine rumbled, and the exhausts made that throaty grumbling noise he liked so much.

"Gimme a minute to get dressed, okay."

"Fine."

"You bounce that thing off my house again, I'm gonna slash your fucking tyres."

"Don't forget to check the stove and unplug your iron," said Junior sweetly. He hit the button and the fast-rising wall of tinted glass pushed Mannie's head back out of the car. Mannie's lips started moving but Junior couldn't hear what he was saying because of the soft, whispering drone of the air-conditioner. Ignoring Mannie, he leaned sideways in his seat and picked up a sheet of pink construction paper from the storage shelf beneath the glove compartment.

Junior's large blunt fingers were not nearly so agile as Misha's, and the origami raccoon was fairly complex by his standards of accomplishment. He had to think carefully about what he was doing, concentrate hard as he folded the stiff square of paper over and over again.

Gradually, the little animal took shape: became a creature of sharp folds and many overlapping angles; planes of shadow and light that shifted constantly as Junior turned the pink paper this way and that, trying, as Misha had taught him, never to stop moving, never to be still.

Mannie's knuckles cracked against the glass. Junior didn't react. He worked at the paper, teasing it out, giving bulk to the raccoon's body. Finally he tossed the finished animal on the dashboard and unlocked the door. Mannie slid into the car. He was wearing a wheat-coloured jacket over a dark green shirt. His pale green slacks were held up by a white leather belt with a big brass buckle that exactly matched the buckles on his pointy white leather shoes. The polished brass accentuated the seven chunky gold rings Mannie was wearing – three on his left hand and four on his right.

"Nice outfit," said Junior.

Mannie nodded, accepting his due. He shut the car door and adjusted his slacks to minimize wrinkling, reached behind him to fasten his seat-belt.

"You buy the shoes and belt at the same time?" said Junior.

"Yeah."

"What're those little red things on your shirt, triangles?"

"Arrowheads."

Mannie flicked a speck of lint from the cuff of his jacket. He stared straight out the windscreen as Junior backed the Trans Am across the lawn, punched another jagged hole in his picket fence. Junior glanced at him, grinning, but Mannie didn't say anything. He marked it down in the big ledger of his mind, though. Junior's time would come. And when it did, Mannie would happily slash his tyres and then slash his fucking throat.

Junior drove down Main and then along Hastings, mile upon mile of depressing architecture and bright red lights. They crept past the south flank of the PNE. It was the second day of the combined exhibition and fair, and there were auxiliary cops everywhere, tied by electric umbilical cords to the metal boxes that controlled the traffic lights. The sidewalks and intersections were thick with people. Junior stared at the women, at the bits and pieces of them that interested him the most. "You ever been to the PNE?" he asked Mannie.

"When I was a kid." Mannie shifted in his seat. He remembered riding the ferris wheel to the top and then throwing pea gravel down at the crowd far below him. People looking up, bewildered.

They crawled past the rotting hulk of Empire Stadium, the heroic Jack Harman bronze of Bannister and Landy breaking the four-minute mile. Junior made a left on Cassiar. The traffic began to clear as they approached the Second Narrows Bridge. Far below them a stiff breeze turned the inlet into a broad field of shattered glass that reflected a million brilliant shards of light. Off to the left were the dull bulk of the grain elevators, acres of neatly stacked lumber, a huge cone of bright yellow sulphur. Dozens of piers thrust the blunt, grasping fingers of commerce into the harbour. And the mountains loomed over everything, bluish-green in the gathering haze.

As they crested the span of the bridge, Junior hit a button and powered open the sunroof. The sudden wind buffeted Mannie, made a ruin of his carefully arranged hair. He lifted his hands to his head, crouched a little lower in his seat.

Junior laughed. "Don't worry about it. It's the natural look."

"I should've worn a suit," said Mannie.

"What for? You're going to brunch, not a fucking funeral."

"I notice you're wearing one."

"That's because I'm working, stupid." Junior took a quick look in his rearview mirror and abruptly changed lanes. The Trans Am fishtailed crazily. The bridge railings whizzed by. Junior seemed unconcerned. "In fact," he said, "if I were you, I'd lose the tie."

"Why, what's wrong with it?"

"Felix and Misha are Californians, Mannie. Very relaxed people. You're gonna be eating out on the patio by the pool. In the backyard, you see what I mean? They're gonna be wearing old cut-offs and those Japanese sweatshirts with messages on 'em nobody can read."

Mannie waited just long enough to let Junior know he wasn't being pushed into anything, and then removed his tie.

"And another thing," said Junior. "Take my advice and never wear green again."

"Why not?"

"Because it ain't your colour, Mannie. Green tints your skin and makes you look dead."

Mannie twisted in his seat. "You trying to tell me something?"

"If I was, you'd be riding in the boot, leaking blood all over my spare tyre."

The Trans Am quivered as the bridge ended and the surface of the road changed from concrete to asphalt. They were on the highway now, in the outside lane, moving west at a steady eighty miles an hour. Mannie stared thoughtfully at the multi-coloured paper zoo crowding the dashboard, pressing up against the windscreen. The mob of miniature beasts was dancing on tiny pointed feet, whipped into a frenzy by the wind from the sunroof. Junior and his origami, mumbo-jumbo about penetrating the Jap psyche. Mannie couldn't even tell what most of the animals were. He liked the alligators, though. And the storks. But most of it was crap. Reaching out, he plucked what might have been an elephant from the frantic, vibrating throng. There was something different about the animal. Unlike its companions, it was a two-tone. Yellow and green.

Mannie saw that it had been fashioned out of a parking ticket.

"Good, huh?" said Junior.

"Terrific," said Mannie. Junior was wearing a vested black suit, white shirt, floppy black bow-tie and a pair of gleaming white Converse Hi-Toppers. He looked like a pallbearer at a funeral for Woody Allen.

But Woody hadn't done anything to annoy Felix Newton, and Mannie had.

By the time the gleaming black nose of the Trans Am turned into Felix's driveway, Mannie's pear-shaped body was wet with fear.

How had he gotten himself into this mess? How was he going to get himself out?

25

Mannie stood on the front porch with the posture of an apprentice vacuum-cleaner salesman while Junior unlocked the big front door with a shiny brass key that must have weighed half a pound. In they went, Junior leading Mannie past a wide spiral staircase and down a long hallway with a glossy parquet floor. Junior's Hi-Toppers chirping and squeaking, making little Trans Am sounds on the polished wood.

Mannie paused to pluck a rose from a slim vase resting in the centre of a graceful inlaid table with bow legs. Junior watched Mannie slip the rose into his jacket lapel. He shook his head, grinning. They went through an open doorway and down three steps into a sunken living-room about twenty feet wide by forty feet long. There was a very large and very valuable Persian rug on the floor, a nice mix of antique furniture. The room was dominated by a huge Sylvania television that squatted on an oval coffee table by the red brick fireplace, in front of a flimsy-looking Queen Anne chair.

The dining-room was off to Mannie's left, and three steps up. On either side of the stairs there were low brick dividers with a profusion of plants growing out of them. The table was laid for twelve, and was awash in glittering silverware, crystal bowls of fresh-cut flowers. The wall behind the table was plate glass; a series of sliding glass doors. Outside, Felix Newton and Misha were sitting at a round metal table in the shade of a big pink-and-white-striped umbrella. They were drinking white wine on the rocks out of oversized glasses. Misha was holding her glass in both hands. Neither she nor Felix noticed Mannie.

"Sit," said Junior.

Mannie looked at him, not quite sure he'd heard him right. Junior pointed at the Queen Anne chair in front of the Sylvania. There was something in Junior's hand. A small, black, rectangular object. Slowly, Mannie lowered himself into the chair.

"Don't move," said Junior. "Stay right where you are."

"Fine with me," said Mannie. He had decided that the black object in Junior's hand was a purse gun, maybe a .25 calibre automatic. Something that would only make little holes in the Persian carpet. He crossed his legs. Now the throwing knife in the ankle sheath was only inches from his hand, a fraction of a second away from Junior's heart.

Junior jogged diagonally across the carpet, up the steps to the dining-room. Mannie saw dark, rippling, distorted bits and pieces of him reflected in the silver as he circumnavigated the table. Then he was out on the patio, leaning over the round metal table, the upper half of his body in the shade of the umbrella. Mannie watched him put the small black rectangle down in front of Felix Newton. Felix turned slightly in his chair, glanced at Mannie without meeting his eyes. He said something to Misha that made her smile, then picked up the black thing and pointed it in Mannie's direction, pressed a button.

The Sylvania came to life, the screen filling with a tight shot of a woman's face. Her lips moved but there was no sound. She smiled, and then her face went out of focus, dissolved into a pink oval as the brand name of a well-known feminine hygiene product was superimposed upon it. Mannie finally noticed the tangle of wires leading from the back of the TV to a video machine squatting on the carpet beneath the coffee table. He uncrossed and then recrossed his legs. Cleared his throat. He was pretty sure he knew what was coming up next, what the feature attraction was going to be.

A free-form blob of polished silver that metamorphosed into the radiator of the Econoline van. A thin woman in designer glasses and a pageboy haircut. Blah blah blah. The two cops. Blah blah blah. Then the part Mannie always looked forward to, the camera moving in on the van, actually getting inside. Red shag. The shards of mirror; Cheshire grins in the quartz lights. Pools of blood. The tooth marks on the back of the bucket seat.

No sound, though.

Junior said something to Felix. The Econoline was sharp and clear and then suddenly juddering, multiple overlapping images of black on black.

Felix had pushed the pause button. Now rewind. A blur of pale green.

Stop.

Forward. This time around, Mannie was privileged to sit through the feminine hygiene commercial from beginning to end before the little drama in the park got underway. Felix kept adjusting the volume, turning it higher and higher, until the speakers started to rattle and the voices were so distorted that Mannie wouldn't have known what people were saying if he hadn't already heard it dozens of times before.

Felix showed him the tape a third time.

And again.

And once more, in slow motion this time, the voices seeming to come from deep under water. Mannie finding himself anticipating questions, rushing ahead of the conversation, guessing a word wrong here and there but mostly getting it right.

Felix gave him the sanitary napkin pitch one last time and killed the picture. Mannie stared at the blank screen for a moment, then reluctantly turned to look out at the sun-bleached patio.

Junior was standing in the open doorway, waving him over. His right arm hung at his side, weighed down by his Colt, the .357 Magnum with the ribbed and ventilated nine-inch barrel.

Mannie stood up. "Where's the bathroom?" he said.

Junior pointed with the gun.

26

Willows got into a firing stance. He pressed his cheek against the polished wooden stock of the rifle, aimed carefully and squeezed the trigger.

The air rifle burped. A froth of water erupted around the leading duck in the back row. Willows heard the sound of pellets hitting tin. The duck fell over on its side and abruptly disappeared beneath the choppy surface of the water.

Willows had the hang of it now. He started letting off single shots, picking his targets with a marksman's skill, tracking the rusty metal birds in his sights as they moved from stage left to stage right.

Sean was laughing; an eight-year-old delighted by his father's skill. But Annie was looking away, making no attempt to hide her disapproval. At the age of eleven, she was very much her mother's daughter – blessed by some prejudices and burdened by others. Willows wondered how much Sheila had told the girl, what she'd said to explain or justify Willows' sudden departure. He put the empty airgun down on the counter. "What next, Annie? Any requests?"

She shrugged disinterestedly. "Not really."

Willows looked down the length of the gallery. "I wonder if we should phone the SPCTA," he said.

"What's that?" said Sean.

Willows smiled. "The Society for the Prevention of Cruelty to Tin Animals." He glanced at his daughter, gave a vaudeville wink.

Annie giggled, her bad mood dissolving into laughter. "Can we go for a ride on the giant rollercoaster?"

Willows made a face, miming abject fear.

"You promised to take me on the bumper cars," said Sean. "Remember?"

Willows nodded.

"The bumper cars are miles away," said Annie. She made a

sweeping gesture with her arm, and then frowned. "What's the matter, you afraid of the rollercoaster?"

"No way," said Sean firmly. He took a bite out of his corn dog. "Dad promised, that's all."

"Why don't we go on the rollercoaster first, since it's closer. Then we can ride the bumper cars. Okay?"

"I guess so," said Sean. He took another bite out of his corn dog, gnawed at the stick and growled low in his throat.

Annie rolled her eyes in mock disgust.

Hand in hand, the three of them walked slowly down the midway, making their way through the bright lights and the noise, the jostling, distracted crowds.

A skinny kid wearing a faded black T-shirt and jeans held up by a length of motorcycle drive-chain lowered a metal safety-bar, slapped it with the heel of his hand to make sure it was locked into place. He grinned down at Willows. "Lucked out, eh? Got yourself the best seats in the house."

Willows glared at him, and the kid moved on.

They were sitting in the front row of the lead car, with nothing in front of them but narrow gauge track: twin bands of polished steel that climbed alarmingly towards the bright blue sky. It was so cramped that his knees touched the metal bulkhead. He sat up a little straighter, trying without success to find more room for his legs. The car lurched forward. He put his arms around his children, braced himself. Sean moved an inch or two away, asserting his independence. They climbed slowly upwards, the angle of ascent gradually becoming steeper.

At the top of the incline the rollercoaster seemed to hesitate, as if balanced precariously on the fulcrum of the track. Willows looked down at the abandoned, rotting hulk of Empire Stadium. He'd won a shiny red ribbon there a quarter of a century ago, for placing third in a high school track meet. His time had been four minutes thirteen seconds. Not quite good enough to get him cast in bronze, but like Landy and Bannister, he'd given it everything he had. He smiled, remembering the scattered applause when he'd stepped up on the rostrum to accept his prize.

"What are you thinking about, Daddy?" said Annie.

136

"My misspent youth," Willows replied. He had no time to explain because suddenly they were plunging down the track, swaying violently from side to side, the wheels thundering beneath them, their eyes filling with tears, Annie's new dress billowing and her hair streaming out behind.

They hit the valley with a jolt. Willows felt the safety-bar press hard against his stomach. Somewhere behind him a girl screamed. Then they were shooting back up again, momentum carrying them effortlessly towards the horizon, the complex of metal girders on either side a dizzy, sickening blur.

Willows tried closing his eyes, but that only made it worse.

At the top of the rise, the track turned sharply left. The blunt nose of the rollercoaster jutted out into space, and for a wild fraction of a second, Willows thought they were going to crash. He was vaguely aware of Annie searching his face for reassurance, and tried to smile. Then they were yanked sideways, tearing around a long, steeply banked curve. Sean flung his arms up in the air. The wind tore at the sleeves of his shirt, made a ripping sound. Willows resisted an impulse to shout at the boy. He held him a little more tightly instead, acutely aware of the small, fragile bones beneath his son's flesh.

The nose dipped and down they went again, but much faster this time. A lot of people were screaming now. He couldn't tell if they were having fun or genuinely frightened. He knew how he felt, though.

Like someone who's just discovered an important phobia.

The rollercoaster ride lasted only a few minutes, but by the time it ended Willows felt he'd more than had his money's worth. Standing on the platform beside the track, he flexed his knees and tried not to feel old.

"Now can we go on the bumper cars?" said Sean.

Willows glanced at his watch. It was half-past-two. He'd had a light breakfast and no lunch, and he was hungry.

"Let's get something to eat," he said.

Sean started to launch into a complaint, had second thoughts. "Can we have a pizza?"

"Sure."

"And cokes?" said Annie.

"Whatever you like."

"I wouldn't mind sitting down for a couple of minutes, anyway," Sean said.

Willows could relate to that. Since they'd entered the fairgrounds they'd had rides on most of the wildlife and all of the major household appliances known to man; laughed at each other's distorted images in the Hall of Mirrors; shrieked with fear and delight in the Tunnel of Doom – and spent at least ninety per cent of their time waiting in line-ups. The experience was remarkably similar to being on a stake-out: long interminable periods of enforced inactivity followed by a few brief moments of intense excitement. If you were lucky.

Not that the children had complained. They seemed to take the delays for granted, and Willows for the most part was content simply to be with them, to share whatever small joys or sorrows the day might bring.

At one of the dozens of tiny take-out restaurants scattered thoroughly about the fairground, Willows ordered a Greek salad and slices of pineapple pizza from a woman in her fifties who seemed to be naked under her faded lime-green overalls.

"It's the heat from the ovens," she said, catching him looking. "Want anything to drink?"

"A large coffee and two small cokes."

The woman reached under the counter for a small, prefolded lidless cardboard box, used her thumb and forefinger to make the sides snap up into place. Willows watched her fill the box with pizza and salad and soft drinks. There was a stack of paper napkins on the counter. He took three. The woman picked up the chewed stub of a pencil, jotted some figures down on a scrap of paper, frowned.

"That'll be seven-fifty."

Willows handed her a ten-dollar bill and pocketed his change. Annie and Sean had laid claim to a nearby table. He sat down, distributed the food.

"You get any straws?" said Sean.

"They didn't have any."

"Did you ask?"

"No, I looked."

"Mom always gets us straws."

"She does not," said Annie, moving in fast.

Willows nibbled at his slice of pizza. It tasted even worse

138

than it looked. He shovelled some salad on to his plate with a plastic fork.

"You can have mine too, if you want it," said Sean. He licked tomato sauce from his fingers, making a big production of it.

"Gross," said Annie. She made a face.

Sean smacked his lips, grinned. "Can I have some candy floss for dessert?"

"Sure, if you eat some salad." Willows toyed with the empty cardboard box. The design was simple but elegant. He caved in the sides, popped them open. Why was he so interested? He pushed the box away.

Annie slid along the bench seat, moving closer. "Can I ask you something, Daddy?"

"What's that, honey?"

"How come you moved out of the house?"

Even though he'd known it was coming, the question still took Willows by surprise. He looked across the table at Sean. The boy was playing with his fork, intent on measuring the tensile strength of the plastic tines.

"Have you talked to your mother about this?" said Willows carefully.

Annie nodded.

"What did she say?"

"That you spent too much time at work and not enough time with your family. That it wasn't fair and she wasn't going to put up with it any more."

No news there.

Willows shredded a paper napkin, balling up the torn fragments of paper and tossing them at his coffee cup. He was keeping himself occupied while waiting for his daughter to unburden herself. It was a cop's trick; a way of downplaying extended silences, easing the pressure. He'd used it in the interrogation room at 312 Main more times than he could remember. He flipped another ball of paper at the cup. It didn't occur to him that his eight-year old son was playing a variation of the same theme.

Annie took a deep breath, let it out. "I told her I'd rather see you a little bit than not at all. I told her I loved you, Daddy. And that I missed you a whole lot."

Willows couldn't think of a single thing to say. He reached out and his daughter threw herself into his arms, her eyes bright with tears.

"Are you ever coming home, Daddy?"

"I hope so, Annie." Willows swallowed, tasted his grief. "I miss you too, you know. I miss all of you, miss you very much. But right now, your mother needs some time to herself."

"Why?"

Willows handed Annie the tattered remains of his napkin. "Because she has to have a chance to think about things and decide how she feels about them," he said. He took the napkin from Annie's restless hands and gently dried her cheeks. "I have to give her as much time as she wants, honey. It isn't easy to explain, but that's the way it is."

"Adult talk," said Annie derisively.

"That's right," said Willows, although in truth he had no more idea what was going on than she did.

The fork snapped with a dry, brittle sound. Pieces of white plastic scattered across the table like the shattered bones of a small animal.

"Sorry," said Sean, grim-faced.

Willows playfully flicked a piece of plastic back at him. He stood up. "Let's get out of here, okay? Let's go get ourselves a face full of candy floss, and then let's grab some wheels and kick ass!"

"Kick what?" said Annie, looking shocked.

"That's Formula One talk," said Willows. "Bumper Car lingo."

"Swearing, if you ask me."

"Kick ass!" yelled Sean.

The woman in the lime overalls gave her counter a quick wipe with a damp cloth and leant out to see what was going on. Willows waved hello and, after a moment's hesitation, she smiled and waved back at him.

"I'm so embarrassed," said Annie.

Willows gave her a sweeping bow. "Allow me to apologize," he said, "by treating you to a bouquet of candy floss."

Annie thought about it for about two seconds and then said, "Pink or blue?"

"Your choice, of course."

"Pink."

27

Mannie was waved into the only chair at the patio table that wasn't shaded by the pink-and-white striped umbrella. He sat down, the hot, flimsy metal creaking under his weight. Felix was wearing a California Angels baseball cap, a pair of cheap rubber thongs, baggy white trousers and a fruit cocktail shirt. Misha sat on Felix's left. She had on a pair of outsized aviator glasses with mirrored lenses, a bikini that looked as if it was made of mauve Teflon. Junior had gone back into the house. Now he came out again, carrying a huge glass bowl full of mixed vegetables.

"You ever read Steinbeck?" said Felix to Mannie.

"Who?"

Ice clinked against Felix Newton's teeth as he sipped at his wine. "What'd you think of the tape?"

Mannie didn't know what to say. He managed a shrug.

"Ninety seconds," said Felix.

"Huh?"

Misha turned towards Mannie, cocked her head to the side, sunlight bouncing off her glasses into his eyes. He looked away, at the pink, heart-shaped pool that dominated the yard.

"Ninety seconds is what they gave your little caper on the eleven o'clock news," said Felix.

"Junior set up the Econoline. It was that fucking bordello on wheels caught everybody's attention."

"Station got a news team out there pretty fast," said Felix. "Cop leaning over a body makes a nice change from some stiff reading a prepared statement from behind a desk, eh?"

"I guess so," said Mannie uncertainly.

"You phone 'em?"

"Who, the cops?"

"No, Mannie. The TV folks."

"Jesus! No, of course not." The late-morning sun beat down on Mannie's scalp, He wiped sweat from his forehead. Felix

Newton was staring at him again, the eyes dark and the heavily lined face without expression.

"Everything's ready to go," said Junior.

Misha looked up at him, her mouth small and annoyed. She pushed herself away from the table, went over to the barbecue. Mannie heard the sound of metal on metal and then a sharp hiss. The sweet scent of melting butter mixed it up with the acrid smell of chlorine from the pool, and lost.

Junior was hovering, trying to decide whether or not to sit down in Misha's vacated chair. Felix snapped his fingers at him. "I got a few things I have to say to Mannie. Go swim some laps."

"Okay," said Junior. He unbuttoned his suit jacket and drew the Colt .357, laid it down on the table next to Felix's wine glass. His Hi-Toppers sucked at the tiles as he ambled towards the pool.

"Shit," said Felix softly. He waited until the last possible moment and then shouted, "Hold it right there!"

Misha had been cracking eggs, but now she stopped. Everybody watched Junior teeter on the lip of the heart-shaped pool, his arms windmilling as he fought to keep his balance.

"That's a three-hundred-dollar suit," Felix yelled. "Take it off, stupid! And while you're at it, get rid of those shoes. You sound like a fucking octopus, creeping around in those things."

Mannie reached across the table and poured himself a glass of white wine. He licked condensation from the glass and took a big gulp. Junior undressed quickly. His stomach looked like a washboard. He bent and unlaced the running shoes, pulled off his socks and stepped out of his pants. Mannie saw that he was tanned all over. His ass was as brown as the rest of him. Was that what they did in California, walk around nude all the time? Junior's hard muscular body arced and he vanished beneath the pink surface of the water. Mannie counted to a hundred and fifty. Junior surfaced, rolled over on his back like a seal. He floated in the middle of the heart, eyes closed, his penis and testicles bobbing gently.

Felix pulled a pack of Camel cigarettes out of his shirt pocket, shook one free and lit up.

"I heard the kid looked as if a shark had got him," he said. "That was dumb. Naomi Lister, on the other hand, was very smart. Some cop fishing way up there in the mountains. Fucking needle in a haystack. But what the hell, right? Two down and one to go. All that counts is the bottom line." Delicately, with his little finger, he flicked ash from his cigarette. "Want to know what this is all about?"

"Not really," said Mannie.

"Junior picked some kids up off Davie Street. Four of 'em. Brought them up here for a party. You know how these things can get out of hand?"

Felix was looking at him, waiting.

"Sure," said Mannie, although he had no idea what they were talking about.

Felix paused while Misha put plates down on the table. Translucent white china with gold trim. An omelette on one side, salad heaped on the other. Felix speared a chunk of tomato, skewering it on the tines of an Art Deco fork.

"I strangled one of them. And Junior got it all down on videotape. At least, the dumb shit thinks he did. When the survivors took off, the tape went with them."

"They try to get in touch with you?"

"We got in touch with them first." Felix frowned. "Can you imagine how I felt about killing that poor kid, when I finally sobered up enough to examine my emotions? Knowing his pals were going to have to go too, because I'm a tidy person and I worry a lot."

"Bad?" said Mannie.

"A flair for understatement. Very rare in a Jewish person." Felix's mouth was full of egg. He stopped talking long enough to swallow. "Junior went through Steve and Naomi's apartment. Nothing there but a bunch of cockroaches. So he drove his fucking Trans Am up to Squamish and tossed her dad's place. Zilch. If anybody's got my tape, it has to be Carly."

"Makes sense," said Mannie.

"You think so, huh? Then why haven't you been out on the street looking for her?"

Mannie shrugged. He toyed with his omelette, pushed a piece of mushroom around the circumference of his plate. "I don't know, it seemed like a good idea to let things cool down a little."

"Seemed like a good idea to you, is that what you mean?"

Felix stabbed viciously at another chunk of tomato. He chewed vigorously. A gelatinous glop of juice and seeds dribbled down his chin. He wiped it away with the back of his hand, licked himself clean.

"Carly's staying with a gimp named Walter. Skinny little guy used to be a jockey."

"Oh yeah, what's he do now?"

"Fences stuff. Mostly junk. Don't worry about it, he's got no connections whatsoever."

Mannie drained his glass. Felix poured him a refill, waved the empty bottle expansively at the city and ocean glittering far below them. "Nice, huh?"

"Really nice," said Mannie.

"Laguna Beach is better, though. Down there, you got weather like this all year round. And where else can you shoot whales from your front porch?" Felix leaned across the table and patted Mannie lightly on the shoulder. "Junior's got the address. You do this right, you got his job."

"Oh yeah?"

Felix pointed at Mannie's rings. "What is all that shit, ten carats?" He smiled. "My people live in an eighteen-carat world, Mannie. You want to move up the ladder, you know how to do it."

Mannie looked closely at Felix and saw he wasn't kidding. "After I get Junior's job," he said, "what happens to Junior?"

"Up to you, kiddo."

"I want a new piece, too," said Mannie. And looked surprised. The words had just popped out. He hadn't thought about it at all.

"A gun?" said Felix. He glanced down at the huge chrome-plated Colt lying next to his plate, beside his coffee spoon.

"No," said Mannie. "A wig."

Real hair. Long and thick. Hair that he could wear with confidence in the shower or in the middle of a fucking hurricane. He saw himself down at Laguna Beach, the surf foaming at his knees, a couple of those leggy Californian blondes wrapped all over him. His hair tossed by the offshore breeze. A tan even better than Junior's.

It could all happen. He knew it could. All he had to do was stay lucky and move fast.

28

The ball was painted dark green, with two glossy white stripes. It lay in a hollow, nestled between the roots of a chestnut tree.

The hoop was about twenty feet away on a twisting downhill slope, barely visible behind the spindly green trunks of an intruding clump of vine maple.

Orwell stared down at the ball and considered his options. He could swing under the ball, try to loft it high enough to luck his way through the tangle of the maples. Or he might bounce it off the chestnut, put some spin on the ball and hope for a lucky bounce that would send it curling around the barrier of the trees. Or he could simply play it safe, drive the ball straight ahead and leave his partner, Brynner, an easy shot next time up.

The first two shots were clearly impossible. The third went against his nature. He mulled it over, taking his time.

"Just knock it ahead about five or ten feet" said Brynner, glaring over the bowl of his pipe.

"I can't."

"Why not?" Brynner had intense dark eyes and an unkempt black beard, an unpleasant habit of nibbling furiously at the edges of his moustache.

"Too easy," said Orwell.

"Fucking hell," whispered Brynner, too quietly for anyone but Orwell to hear. "We can win this thing, eh? The whole bag of marbles! All you have to do is quit screwing around."

Orwell took a few practice swings. He shifted his stance minutely and then drew back and hit the ball with all the force and conviction he could muster. It struck the chestnut with a dull thud and shot off at a crazy angle, missing Jerry Goldstein's wife by inches.

"Fore!" yelled Orwell. There was a scattering of laughter.

Brynner chewed at his moustache.

Orwell watched a girl with short red hair line up her shot,

drill her ball thirty feet across uneven ground and right through the heart of the hoop, strike a pose.

"Fuck," said Brynner.

"I'm thirsty," said Orwell. "I think I'll go get something to drink."

"Just don't come whining to me when your kidneys give out and transplant time rolls around."

Orwell looked at Brynner to see if he was kidding. It wasn't possible to say. They were playing the second and final round of the match. Out of sixteen original players, there were only eight left: four teams of two. Orwell silently cursed the luck of the draw. Brynner was not a very amiable person. Orwell had a hunch the guy was out on a day pass from someplace with iron bars on the windows.

He made his way out of the trees, over to where Judith was sitting in the sun in a webbed aluminium lawn chair. She was wearing a wide-brimmed white cotton hat with a scarlet band, a flimsy white summer dress that she'd pulled high on her thighs in order to catch some tan. Orwell sat down next to her on a Coleman cooler. She gave him a big smile.

"Nice stroke, Eddy. If you'd put a little more weight behind it, you might've killed her."

"Scare tactics, that's all. You cripple one of 'em, the rest fall into line real fast."

Judith was cradling a bottle of cheap white wine in her lap. Orwell watched her fumble with the screw cap, take a hit. Screw the cap back on. He held out his hand and she passed the bottle to him. He took a sip. The wine was lukewarm, brackish.

"Brynner keeps making these incredibly rotten shots. So I end up looking like a dunce, trying to get out of all the jams he leaves me in. How we ever made it through the first round is something I'll never know."

"The rest of us deliberately blew it so we could settle down to some serious drinking," said Judith. The chair creaked as she leaned towards Orwell to retrieve the bottle.

"Brynner's about as much fun as a fucking bunion. If I was a quitter, I'd quit right this minute."

"You can always turn into a quitter, Eddy. You know what they say, it's never too late to change."

Impulsively, Orwell reached out and squeezed Judith's hand. "I'd like to quit being a bachelor," he said. "Why don't we get married."

"Who to?" said Judith, drawing back.

"Each other, for Christ's sake!"

Orwell got down on his knees. He pulled the sterling silver box out of his trouser pocket, flipped up the lid. The diamond, a half carat of pure carbon crystallized in regular octahedrons and allied forms, caught the light and flashed sparks of red and green.

"Say no!" someone shouted from the trees. There was a burst of laughter.

Orwell flushed. He thrust the ring towards Judith. "Say yes," he said. "Please say yes."

Judith tried the ring on. It fit surprisingly well. She slipped it off her finger, put it back in the silver box. "You're the second man to ask me to marry him this week," she said.

Orwell stared at her. "I am?"

"Parking violation. Meter had run out. The guy showed up just as I was sticking the ticket under his windscreen wiper. Said he'd been waiting for me all morning long."

"Oh yeah? and he asked you to marry him?"

Judith nodded. She drank deeply of the wine, holding the bottle in both hands. When she was finished drinking she put the bottle down on the grass and moved her chair around a few degrees. Orwell's first thought was that she wanted to face him more directly, but then he realized she was simply chasing the sun.

"He figured if we were married he'd be able to beat the ticket because I wouldn't be able to testify against him in court." Judith picked up the bottle and drank another inch. "A real kidder, a genuine comedian."

"What'd you say?"

"I told him he needed a better reason than that, and so did I. You know what happened?"

"No, what?"

"He grabs the ticket and turns it into a cute little paper elephant. With a trunk, and ears that stick way out, stumpy legs and everything."

"He turned the parking ticket into an elephant?"

"You should've seen his hands, Eddy. A blur, they moved so fast."

"No shit," said Orwell. He chopped idly at the grass with the head of his mallet, gouging neat crescents out of the lawn. Judith was staring at him, looking at him as if she was waiting for him to say something. He took a few more swipes at the grass and then said, "Hey, wait a minute!"

"What?"

"This is the same guy you gave a ticket to last week, right?"

"That's right, Eddy."

"With the black Trans Am. We were talking about it at the juice bar at the club." Orwell frowned. "The guy said he was waiting for you?"

"He sure did."

"What else did he say?"

"He asked me if I wanted to go for a drive," said Judith. She didn't see any point in telling Orwell where Junior had suggested they go, which was to the Hyatt Regency, or how he'd gone into extremely graphic detail about what he wanted to do to her once they got there. "I told him to forget it, I wasn't interested. He jumped into his big black car with the tinted windows, and took off."

"Mad, huh. Burn a little rubber?"

"All the way down the block."

"Punk. You think there's any chance he might come back?"

"Who can say," said Judith, not sounding too worried about it. She reached down into her bag for a tube of coconut oil. Orwell watched the smooth brown skin of her thigh dimple under the pressure of her fingers.

"What about us?" he said.

"What about you and that cute little brunette detective named Claire Parker?" Judith shot back.

Orwell blushed. "How did you hear about her?"

"Never mind, Eddy."

"I just went out with her a couple of times." He was whining. He cleared his throat, and frowned.

"Three times," said Judith. "You went out with her three times in two weeks. And the last time was to that expensive restaurant in the park, wasn't it?"

"Kearns told you, didn't he?"

"Don't blame your partner for your troubles, Eddy. Blame yourself."

"It wasn't anything serious. It was a last fling, that's all. I mean, I didn't ask *her* to marry me, did I."

Somebody tapped him on the shoulder. It was Brynner, his dark eyes glistening. "Your shot," he said. "You two getting hitched?"

"I doubt it," said Judith. She applied a little more coconut oil. "I'm going to have to think about it," she said. "It's a nice diamond, but I'd never want to be a man's second choice.'

"Good for you," said Brynner.

Orwell struggled to his feet. There were grass stains on the knees of his white trousers. He twirled the croquet mallet in his hands, and glared at Brynner as if he was lining up his next shot, and Brynner's bald head was the ball. Chewing on his moustache, Brynner slowly backed away.

29

Willows borrowed the Duty Sergeant's Bic pen and signed an unmarked chocolate-brown Ford Fairlane out of the car pool. He checked to make sure the cherry and the radio and the computer terminal worked, then wheeled out of the parking lot and on to Cordova.

He drove down Cordova for three blocks, turned right on Jackson, made a quick left on Prior and accelerated up the concrete access ramp to the Dunsmuir Viaduct. Almost directly ahead of him the bloated, bone-white fibreglass roof of the domed stadium rose up to dominate the south-west quadrant of the city's skyline. Off to his right, the old *Vancouver Sun* building looked as if it was waiting to be climbed by a giant ape.

It was Monday night, a few minutes past ten. The temperature was in the high seventies, and holding steady. There was a breeze coming in from the ocean; the air smelled of iodine. Traffic was moderate.

On the downtown core side of the viaduct Willows impatiently waited out a red light and then turned on to Howe Street, one of the main arteries that skirted the city's financial district. He drove one short block down Howe and hit another red. As he sat in the idling Ford waiting for the light to change, he was suddenly filled with a sense of urgency and despair. Too much time had passed since the discovery of the bodies of Naomi Lister and her still-unidentified boyfriend. The vast majority of murder cases were solved in the first few days of the investigation or not at all. This one was slipping away from him, fading fast.

At the corner of Robson and Davie, Claire Parker sat at a bus stop bench drinking grape juice out of a waxed cardboard carton, and reading the graffiti spray-painted all around her. Willows pulled the Fairlane tight against the curb and Parker stood up. She opened the Fairlane's door and slid inside, adjusted her skirt. She shut the door and said, "Let's roll, partner!"

Willows just sat there, not moving. Parker was wearing a dark blue skirt and matching jacket, a creamy white blouse with an open neck. She drank the last of the grape juice and reached out the window and tossed the container into a litter bin. Willows still hadn't moved. She turned to him and said, "Something wrong, Jack?"

"No, not a thing. I was just admiring your outfit. Nice suit. Very businesslike. Makes you look like a lawyer."

Parker shrugged. "Eddy Orwell took me out to dinner."

"Lucky you."

"Have you ever been up on top of the Sears Building, that revolving tower?"

Willows shook his head. "No, I can't say I have."

"Real nice view," said Parker, doing her best to mimic Orwell's gravelly voice.

"I can imagine."

"What Eddy kept wondering about, all through the meal, was the plumbing. How do they keep the pipes from getting all twisted up? When you flush the toilet, where does it all go? Fascinating." Parker tilted the rearview mirror towards her, peered intently at her reflection. "Tell me something, Jack. Do you think I'm too old for Eddy?"

"Everybody over the mental age of twelve is too old for Eddy." Willows swung the mirror back into position, twisted in his seat to check the traffic, and hit the gas. "Why, did he give you the brush-off?"

"I'm a free woman," said Parker. "No encumbrances."

Willows let that one go by.

The Fairlane was burning oil and the automatic transmission was out of adjustment, the bands were slipping. They were cruising down the twelve-hundred block Davie, between Bute and Jervis. There were hookers everywhere. Space was at a premium, the intersections filled to capacity, groups of two or three prostitutes at every corner. As they drove west, down the slope towards English Bay, the women faded and the boys took over. They looked right through the Fairlane. The four doors and blackwall tyres made the car instantly recognizable as a police vehicle – the two small whip antennae sticking out of the boot were simply icing on the cake.

Willows drove past Jervis and pulled up next to a fireplug halfway down the block. A street-cleaning machine sloshed up the hill towards them, huge brushes spinning, jets of water spraying both sides of the street, sluicing the day's accumulation of filth into the gutters. Willows turned off the engine. He rolled up his window and waited until the big white machine had roared past, then pushed open his door and got out of the car. The wet and steaming asphalt was a palette of colour – blurred smears of neon pinks, greens and blues.

"All set?" said Parker.

Willows reached under his jacket and shifted the angle of his .38 snubbie in its clamshell holster. He got out of his car and slammed the door shut, then examined his reflection in the car window, making sure that his jacket hung properly and that the gun didn't show.

The two detectives strolled up the sidewalk, Parker adjusting to Willows' slow, rolling gait, the pace he'd learned during his years as a uniformed patrolman.

The experience they had with two women in front of the government liquor store on Alberni was typical in most respects of the way things had been going, and the way they went that night.

The women were both hungry. It is not against the law in Canada to be a prostitute, but it is illegal to actively solicit business. Willows watched the women move with the flow of the traffic, all hips and mouths and pouting breasts as they patrolled the curb, smiling sightlessly into the glare of the lights and the glossy metal bodies of the slow-moving cars that cruised past them like the links of an endless chain. He and Parker were about thirty feet away when the nearest of the women noticed them. She said something to her companion and they both began to walk rapidly down the street, heading towards the alley.

"Hold it!" Willows shouted.

The women slowed, glanced uncertainly at each other, stopped.

"It's those six-inch spike heels," said Parker. "If they'd been wearing flats, they'd have run for it."

The women turned to face the approaching cops. A chorus line of two. Twin sisters wearing frilly pink dresses in a clinging, translucent material. Blue nylons sprinkled with tiny silver stars. Hair cut short and ragged, dyed blonde with streaks of red and green and purple. Eyes sunk deep in blue shadow, cheeks heavily rouged, lips blood-red and glistening.

Willows found himself staring. He was looking at a pair of Shirley Temple clones created by a mad scientist in a late-night movie. The women stared back at him with knowing, half-bright eyes. If there was going to be a conversation, he'd have to start it. He took the morgue shot of Naomi Lister out of his shirt pocket, held it up so it was illuminated by the light from the liquor store window. "Do either of you know this girl?" he said.

The women edged a little closer, curious. Willows saw they weren't sisters after all, they were just dressed to look that way. Both of them were about the same age, though, early twenties. The woman on his right was plump, almost chubby. Her fingernails were bitten to the quick. Her companion had a small scar high up on her neck, just beneath the lobe of her ear. The roots of her hair were black. She rested a hand lightly on Willows' arm.

"What do you want her for? What'd she do?"

"Nothing," said Willows.

"Yeah, right. That explains why you're so interested in her."

"What's the girl's name?" said the plump woman. She was looking at Parker.

"Naomi Lister."

The woman studied the passing traffic, and then said, "I've seen her around. Not lately, though. Two or three weeks ago, maybe a month. She in some kind of trouble, her parents looking for her?"

Parker glanced at Willows. Willows nodded.

"She's in the morgue," said Parker. "She's dead."

The woman with black roots fumbled in her purse, pulled out a crumpled pack of Virginia Slims and lit up, blew a stream of smoke at the passing cars.

"You from out of town?" said Willows.

153

"What makes you ask?"

"The cigarettes."

"Aren't you clever. Keep it up, one of these days you might make detective."

"Seattle?"

"Portland."

"What happened to Naomi?" said the plump woman with the chewed fingernails. She was deliberating changing the subject, but Willows didn't mind. The only reason he was hassling the import from Portland was to give her a motive to cooperate.

"Somebody killed her," he said. He took another morgue shot out of his pocket, this one of the boy found stabbed to death in the back of the Econoline. The plump woman glanced at the picture and nodded. "His picture was in the papers, right?"

"You know him?"

"Not really." She paused, and then said, "What're you gonna do about my sister, kick her ass across the border, or what?"

"That depends," said Willows.

The import with the blonde hair and the black roots flicked her cigarette into the gutter. "Talk to him, Shirley, and let's get the fuck out of here."

"I've seen them around," the plump woman said to Parker.

"What, both of them? Naomi *and* the boy?"

"Yeah, that's right. They were living together. Rumour was, they were going to get married." She smiled crookedly. "Cute, huh. I mean, what were they, about ten years old?"

"Wait a minute," said Willows. "I thought the kid was gay."

"Why, just because he did a little business? Don't be so naive, handsome. He was just looking to earn a dollar, that's all."

"Beats pumping gas," said the import.

"What was his name?" said Parker.

The plump woman shook her head. "No idea."

"You know anybody who knew him?" Parker persisted.

"I don't mix with the younger set. It's too depressing. Ask some of the kids his own age, why don't you."

"Good idea," said Willows. He handed the woman his card. The card had his name printed on it, and beneath his name his office and home phone numbers. The home number had been inked out, and the number of his new apartment written beneath it. "If you hear anything, give me a call, okay?"

"Sure thing," said the woman from Portland, already turning away.

"How come you don't have a card?" said the plump woman to Parker.

"He's the card," said Parker. "I'm the serious one."

The woman smiled, not getting it, but trying hard. Her front teeth were stained with lipstick. Parker thought about vampires. "Have a nice evening," she said. The woman made as if to blow her a kiss, but lost her nerve. She hurried after her friend, her heels clicking on the pavement.

"I think she kind of likes you," said Willows.

"Do you blame her?" said Parker. They stared at each other for a moment. Willows blinked first.

At two o'clock in the morning they decided to take a break, and walked over to a nearby twenty-four hour restaurant to take a load off their aching feet and grab a bite to eat. Willows bought himself a large glass of two per cent milk and filled a second glass with water and chipped ice. Parker ordered a cheeseburger and a pot of tea. She scooped some cutlery out of the plastic self-serve bins, and they found a table near the window.

The restaurant was air-conditioned. Willows could feel the sweat cooling on his back. Two o'clock in the morning, and it was still in the mid-seventies. He sipped at his milk, drank a little iced water. He wiped his forehead with a paper napkin, tossed the napkin on the table.

Parker sipped at her tea. "Nobody seems to know these kids," she said to Willows. "It's as if they never existed, and it doesn't make sense. Whoever heard of a juvenile hooker who didn't mingle."

Willows nodded vaguely, not wanting to talk about it. His lungs were clogged with exhaust fumes. He felt tired and dirty. He needed a shower and a couple of inches of Cutty Sark, sleep. He drank a little more milk. "How was the croquet?" he said. "You have a good time?"

"I didn't go. Did you really think I would?"

"No, I guess not."

Parker's number was called over the P.A. System. She

pushed away from the table and went to collect her food. Willows passed the time watching a kid in a sleeveless V-neck sweater and a polka-dot bow-tie amuse his date by walking a quarter across his knuckles. He yawned. What he needed was to lie down somewhere, stretch out and fall asleep, sleep without dreaming. Not at the apartment, though. Nothing depressed him more than unlocking his fireproof metal door and walking into all that silence, even the sound of his breathing absorbed by the empty space and wall-to-wall carpet.

Parker came back to the table carrying a tray loaded down with a huge cheeseburger and a side of French fries, a second pot of tea and a spare plate. Indicating the empty plate, she said, "Have some fries."

"Thanks anyway, I think I'll stick with the milk."

"When was the last time you had a decent meal?" said Parker. "Put some carbohydrates in your stomach, it'll do you good."

"You sound exactly like my grandmother."

Parker smiled. She cut the cheeseburger in half and used the blade of her knife to shovel the burger and a handful of fries on to the empty plate, pushed the plate across the table. "Just don't tell me I look like her."

Willows helped himself to a French fry. It was hot and crisp. Tasty. He took another one, nibbled.

Parker gave the ketchup bottle a thump. "You're losing weight," she said. "You've got to start taking care of yourself."

"Okay," said Willows. He bit into the burger and chewed with mock enthusiasm.

They ate in silence, both of them concentrating on the food. When Parker's plate was clean, she leant back in her seat and poured herself another cup of tea and said, "Did Eddy Orwell mention the tournament to you?"

Willows chewed and swallowed. He had only brought the subject of the tournament up because he was making an effort to avoid discussing the investigation. He had a feeling that if they started talking about the case, pretty soon one of them would admit out loud that they weren't getting anywhere, that they were wasting their time. "No," he said in answer to Parker's question, "Eddy didn't say a thing. In fact, I haven't even seen him for about a week."

"Well, he talked to me about it," said Parker. "When he wasn't philosophizing about the plumbing in the Sears Tower, all he could talk about was his girlfriend, Judith Lundstrom. Have you ever met her?"

"Once."

"What's she like?"

"Very blonde. Not the kind of girl you'd ask for directions to the library."

"At the tournament, Eddy asked her to marry him. She said she'd think about it. She told him he was the second man to propose to her within the week."

Willows ate another French fry. The last thing he wanted to talk about was marriage.

"Last week, Judith gave a guy a parking ticket on Hornby Street, out in front of the Supreme Court. Friday, the guy shows up for another one. The meter's expired, he's waiting in the shrubbery for her to walk by and hang some paper on his windscreen. Told her he thought she was kind of cute, that he wanted to buy her lunch."

"Eddy was pretty upset, was he?"

"What bothered Eddy was that the guy took the parking ticket and turned it into an elephant."

Willows had been chasing a fragment of fried onion around the perimeter of his plate. He put down his fork and said, "You just lost me, Claire."

"What I'm saying is that the guy took the parking ticket and folded it up so it looked like a baby elephant. And the one before that, the first ticket she gave him, he turned into a paper dragon."

"Origami," said Willows.

"That's right, origami." Parker was leaning across the table, staring at him, waiting expectantly.

"I don't get it," said Willows. "What's the point?"

"The night I found the body in the van," said Parker, "a car drove by, a black car, with wide rear lights and a little spoiler, a deep, throaty exhaust. After I talked to Eddy, I asked myself if it could have been a Trans Am. The answer was yes."

Willows had it now. Parker thought there might be a connection between the paper animals and all those unexplained folds and creases in the bloody hundred-dollar bill they'd found in the park. He frowned. It was a long shot, but what else did they have? Nothing.

"Was this Eddy's idea, or yours?"

"Eddy's," said Parker. "He's interested in the case because he was there when I found the body. And I think he's on to something."

"Did Judith tell Eddy what the guy looked like?"

"No, and Eddy didn't ask."

"Why don't we give her a call, and see if we can get a description."

Parker looked at her watch. It was twenty minutes to three.

"Have you got her number?" said Willows.

"Of course not."

"Call Eddy."

"No, I won't. You do it."

Willows stood up and fished in his pockets for a quarter. There was a pay phone over by the door. While he listened to the steady, insistent ringing of Orwell's telephone, he watched the kid with the bow-tie. The boy dropped his coin and had to bend under the table to retrieve it. Willows noted that he took the opportunity to peek up his date's skirt. Feeling old and lonely, Willows looked out through the plate-glass window at the bright and empty streets.

If he didn't want to go back to his apartment tonight, where was he planning to stay? At Claire's? He'd tried that once before. Afterwards, it hadn't seemed like a very good idea.

30

Walter the fence did his business out of a decrepit second-hand store on Lower Lonsdale. The building was two storeys of crumbling grey stucco, with a false front dating from the Twenties. Junior had said Walter lived upstairs, that the top floor had been converted into a three-bedroom apartment.

Mannie checked the plate-glass windows and saw that they were wired. He loitered at the front door. It was fitted with a Grantham deadbolt. Carbon steel, six tumblers.

He went around to the back.

At the rear of the building there was another door, a featureless slab of wood with another Grantham and no door-knob. Mannie gave it a push, gentle but firm. The door was solid as a brick wall.

There was only one window. It was rectangular, about a foot high and twice that wide. Mannie walked down the alley until he found a garbage can. He carried the can back to the building, turned it upside down and climbed on top of it. Now his shoulders were level with the sill. He rubbed a circle of oily grime from the glass and examined the window carefully. It, too, was wired with the silvery alarm tape.

Not to worry.

Mannie's primary weapon was an eight-inch skinning knife with bone grips carved from the ribs of an anaconda. For insurance he carried a pair of throwing knives, one strapped to each ankle. He lifted his right leg and unsheathed the knife, steadied himself by gripping the window-sill with his free hand, and went to work.

The putty was old and crumbly, easily pried away from the frame. In less than half an hour all that was holding the window in place were the points, half a dozen sharp little triangles of glazier's metal that had originally been used to support the glass while it was being puttied. Mannie used the broad, double-edged tip of the knife to remove the points. When he was finished he tapped the sheet of glass and it fell towards him, into his waiting hands.

There was about a foot of slack in the unshielded electrical lead that ran from the silvered tape to the circuit-box screwed to the inside wall. Mannie needed every available inch of it to turn the sheet of glass sideways, so that it jutted out at a right angle from the wall of the building. Balancing it on the sill, he pressed it up against the vertical framework and held it in place with two of the glazier's points. Chunks of loose putty fell from the sill and drummed briefly on the upturned garbage can. Mannie held his breath, waiting.

Silence.

He pushed off against the garbage can, wriggled through the window on his belly, managed to turn over on his back and grab the frame, grunted as he hauled himself the rest of the way inside. He dropped to the floor, staggered but managed to keep his balance, crouched with his hand on the hilt of the skinning knife.

Nothing.

The room was in darkness except for the dim incidental light seeping in through the window. As Mannie's eyes adjusted to the gloom he saw that the room was small, about ten feet square, and that most of the floor space was filled with large wooden packing crates that had been ripped open and were vomiting excelsior and a jumble of shiny new outboard motors. He made his way past the crates to a door on the far side of the room. It was fitted with a Grantham lock identical to the one on the front door, but this time luck and the hinges were on Mannie's side.

It took him two minutes to find the crowbar that had been used to rip open the crates, five more to get the door out of his way.

Once while he was working he heard an odd sound directly above him, a dry clicking like a long row of dominoes falling over. The sound wasn't repeated, and after a thirty-second wait, he went back to work.

Mannie opened the door and found himself behind a sales counter. A sawn-off baseball bat lay on a shelf beneath the open cash-register, empty except for a handful of coins. Mannie instinctively reached out, then let his hand drop. Wouldn't be too smart, creeping around with a bunch of loose change rattling in his pocket.

The bat might come in handy, though. He picked it up. The handle was sticky with electrician's tape. He swung the bat through the darkness in a short, vicious arc.

The stairs were off to his left. He climbed them inch by inch, keeping well to the side, leaning as much of his weight as possible on the bannister.

There was another goddam door at the top of the stairs. Mannie tried the knob. The door swung open.

So easy.

As he shut the door behind him he became aware of a low rumbling, a growl that was almost subsonic. A shadow detached itself from the deeper shadows at the end of the corridor, moved swiftly towards him. He heard more dominoes toppling, identified the tap of claws on a wooden floor.

"Nice dog," he whispered.

The doberman bared its teeth. To Mannie it seemed as if its dark muscular gleaming body was nothing but a large engine designed specifically to propel the dog towards him and power the terrible machinery of its gaping jaws.

He stepped back, crouching low. The creature accelerated, leapt towards him on a trajectory intended to bring its incisors in contact with his jugular.

Mannie straightened and whacked the dog between the ears with the fat of his bat.

The doberman's fangs snapped together with the sound of crockery breaking. Mannie felt its fetid breath on his cheek, bore the weight of the animal as it slid down his chest.

Straddling the brute he swung the bat twice more, then kneeled to rest the palm of his hand against the swell of the ribcage. There was no hint of movement but he struck the dog another blow anyway, for luck.

There was one more door he had to get through. It was at the end of the corridor; a slab of grey-painted steel fitted with the inevitable Grantham and two alarm systems that Mannie could see, probably more that he couldn't. A spyhole was set into the door at eye-level. He took a peek through it but it was like looking down a well. He stood there in the darkened hallway, staring at the dim motionless shape of the dead doberman.

Thinking.

"Arf! Arf!"

No response.

Mannie barked again, louder. He tried a growl and then scratched at the base of the door with his skinning knife, barked some more.

The door opened. A man shaped like a blimp and covered with coarse black hair blinked down at Mannie, his pig eyes registering surprise, puzzlement. The man was naked except for a pair of Jockey shorts and the gun in his right fist.

Mannie kicked him in the shorts and then used the bat on him. A field of blood-red exclamation marks blossomed on the ceiling. The man dropped to his knees and then fell backwards, legs tucked neatly beneath him.

Mannie kicked the door shut and shot the bolt. There was a light in the next room. He went through an arched doorway and found himself in the kitchen.

The light was coming from the refrigerator. Walter the fence was standing in front of the open door with a chicken leg in one hand and an unopened can of beer in the other. He was wearing a pale yellow nightshirt with vertical green stripes. His eyes dropped to the skinning knife. He held up the drumstick as if it had some magic power that would keep Mannie at bay.

"What d'you want?" he said. He peered over Mannie's shoulder and said, "Alvin!"

"Alvin's taking a nap," said Mannie. "Bowser's taking a nap too." He started to move in on Walter. "Now it's your turn."

"Fuck you," said Walter. He threw the full can of beer at Mannie and Mannie swung late. The beer caught him high on the cheekbone. He dropped the bat but kept moving forward. Half-blinded by pain, he took an exploratory swipe with the knife and gouged a curving line of enamel out of the refrigerator door. The chicken leg bounced off his shoulder and then Walter smacked him on the side of the head with a five-pound bag of frozen peas. The bag burst, and Mannie went roller-skating. His feet flew out from under him. He landed on his ass on the linoleum.

Walter started throwing things. More frozen vegetables, an

aluminium tray of ice cubes, cardboard cartons of milk, the rest of the chicken, a dozen eggs, yoghurt, a pound of coffee, more cans of beer, a slab of back bacon, half a lemon meringue pie that hit Mannie square in the face.

A head of lettuce followed, and then a plastic bag of tomatoes, a foot-long English cucumber, limp bundle of celery.

Scattering of radishes.

One wrinkled apple.

Walter swore. In the space of a few short seconds he'd clawed his way from the freezer all the way down to the crisper, and now he was out of ammunition.

Mannie scrambled to his feet. He wiped meringue from his face.

Walter lashed out with a bottle of white wine he'd yanked from a shelf set in the refrigerator door. The bottle struck Mannie on the elbow of his raised left arm; it was a classic defensive wound. Blood bubbled thickly out of a ragged tear in his flesh. He screamed with rage, and stabbed at Walter with the knife. Walter danced away, the yellow nightshirt billowing. He moved in again, slashing at Mannie's eyes with the jagged neck of the bottle. Mannie retreated. Walter skittered sideways, circling to his left. Mannie suddenly understood that all Walter wanted was a way out, to skoot.

He let Walter get himself in line with the door, retreat shuffling through the mess on the floor. When Walter's hopeful face was framed in the doorway, Mannie let him have it.

Walter saw Mannie's arm come up, saw Mannie point dramatically at him as if accusing him of something. At the same instant he felt a blow to his throat, just above the collarbone. He tried to look down. His chin bumped against the stubby hilt of a knife. Blood, hot and viscous, filled his throat and trickled down into his lungs. Gagging, he dropped the broken bottle and fell on his side.

Mannie pushed the refrigerator door open a little more, so the widening beam of light fell across Walter's body.

Walter raised his right arm. He brought his fist down hard, with all the strength that remained in him. A quart of milk exploded in a white froth.

Mannie stumbled through the apartment, turning on lights wherever he came across a switch. Eventually he found the bathroom. He turned on the cold water tap, washed the larger fragments of glass out of his arm and bound the cut with a clean washcloth and a pressure bandage from the medicine cabinet. Walter's estate was further diminished to the tune of five aspirins and several little red pills Mannie ate hoping they might be speed. He'd never before had anybody throw a grocery store at him. It was an experience that took a great deal out of a man. He felt real run-down, in need of a boost.

He sat down on the rim of the bathtub, his head cocked to one side, waiting for the pills to do their stuff. Blood seeped through the pressure bandage. It ran down his arm and across the back of his hand, painted his fingers red and dripped slowly to the floor.

After a little while Mannie gave up on the idea of feeling any better. He staggered back through the apartment and out to the hall, grabbed the stiffening doberman by an ear and hauled it inside the apartment.

Kicked shut the door. Locked it.

His arm ached something fierce. Holding it close to his body, he crossed the living-room and sat down on the chesterfield to wait for the girl, Carly.

Minutes and hours slipped by. He dozed, came half-awake, drifted off again. A car stopped out on the street. Mannie heard a door slam shut. He looked out the window and saw a taxi idling at the curb. As he watched, the roof light came on and the taxi drove away.

He went over to the dead man in the shorts, knelt beside him, lifted his left arm and peered at his watch. It was a few minutes past four o'clock in the morning.

Mannie let the arm drop. He eased the skinning knife out of its sheath and went over to stand beside the door.

In a few minutes Carly would be all his. He told himself not to get excited, not to finish her off until she'd led him to Felix Newton's partytime video cassette. He was looking forward to viewing the tape, punching it into his VCR and settling back with a cold brew and a bowlful of taco chips. If he liked what he saw maybe he'd make a copy. For insurance, just in case Felix took out his pocket calculator and decided it'd be a whole lot more cost-effective to wipe Mannie out than pay him the ten grand he was gonna owe him in about ten seconds.

Mannie heard Carly's heels in the hallway. He tensed, getting set.

Nothing happened. He waited maybe a minute, maybe two. Then he lost patience and slipped the lock and yanked open the door.

When Carly had reached the top of the stairs she'd flipped on the hall light. Where the Doberman had died there was a swamp of blood and faeces. The smell was awful, bad enough to chase the flies away.

Mannie heard a noise downstairs. He went after her, taking the steps two and three at a time, crashing into the darkness with fear and murder in his heart.

31

The City of Vancouver employs ten meter maids to patrol the downtown core. During a typical shift each woman will issue between fifty and eighty tickets; in the course of an average week approximately four thousand individual tickets are written. Computer records are kept and notices of non-payment of fines together with the empty threat of a summons are mailed automatically to the registered owners of offending vehicles. The paper carbons of the original tickets are filed in heavy cardboard cartons in a city-leased warehouse. At the end of four years, unpaid tickets are written off as a bad debt. The paper is recirculated – reduced to pulp.

It took Willows and Parker and the three junior clerks they'd recruited to assist them less than an hour to unearth the second of the tickets Judith Lundstrom had slapped on the windscreen of the black Trans Am.

The two detectives took the ticket back to 312 Main. A priority telex to the Motor Vehicle Branch in Victoria was answered in just under three minutes.

The car was registered in the name of an American woman named Misha Yokóte. Residences were listed as Laguna Beach, California, and 616 Greenbriar Lane, in the nearby municipality of West Vancouver.

"Let's check out Laguna Beach first," joked Parker.

Willows smiled politely, and kept reading. According to the MVB telex, Misha Yokóte was twenty-eight years old, a spinster. She had black hair and brown eyes. Her height was five foot one and she weighed one hundred and four pounds. Miss Yokóte had no visible scars. She was restricted to driving with the aid of corrective lenses. Her British Columbia driver's licence had been issued in June of 1982. It was clean: no wants, no warrants.

"I wonder who's been driving Misha's car," said Parker.

"Let's go see Bradley," said Willows. "If we're going to stake out a West Van address, he's going to have to know all about it."

"And so will the West Van cops."

Willows nodded glumly. West Vancouver had its own police force, and they were responsible for maintaining the peace in an area where the inhabitants were noted for their advanced age and high incomes. Willows had worked with the West Van cops before, and knew that they'd be a lot more concerned with serving their own interests than cooperating with a couple of hotshot dicks from the big city. He folded the telex in half and put it in his wallet.

Bradley moved the area map around on his desk like a shirt on an ironing-board, flattening out the wrinkles with the palm of his hand. He found Greenbriar Lane in the index, then used the coordinates to locate it on the map.

"Nice neighbourhood."

"We'll try not to create a disturbance," said Willows.

"You talk to the West Van cops?"

"We thought we'd let you handle it."

"Thanks a lot, Jack. How many teams are you going to need?"

"We can do it with three."

"If you say so." Bradley studied the map. Ash fell from his cigar, polluting several scale miles of the West Vancouver foreshore. "You can have Farley Spears. I'll try for Ralph Kearns and Eddy Orwell. Orwell's been pushing for a transfer, let's see how he does." He gave Parker a bland, depthless smile. "You're a man short, somebody'll have to double up."

Out in the squad room, the telephone on Willows' desk rang harshly.

"Keep in touch," said Bradley, waving them out of his office.

Willows picked up the phone. It was Pat Rossiter, the Mountie from Squamish.

"Bill Lister, Naomi's father, killed himself first thing this morning," Rossiter said without preamble.

Willows was stunned.

"His gas station opens at seven. The mechanic found him in one of the service bays, sitting in his car. He'd run a hose from the exhaust pipe in through the back window, and gassed himself." Rossiter paused. "You still there, Jack?"

"What else have you got?"

"He wrote a suicide note. A confession. He murdered his daughter."

Willows thought about the carving in Lister's living-room. Christ on the cross, the face twisted in anger.

"The note was hand-written," said Rossiter. "There's no question it's authentic. Lister drove up the mountain in a four-wheel drive Jeep that was in the shop for a lube and oil, and a new section of exhaust pipe."

Willows nodded into the phone. He was thinking about the smear of fresh grease he'd found in the grass by the creek, the traces of carbon-monoxide poison in Naomi Lister's blood.

"Bill Lister wrote down the Jeep owner's name. We checked the work records. The vehicle was left at the station on August thirteenth, and picked up three days later. The owner was down in Seattle for a dirty weekend with his girlfriend."

"You talked to him?"

"Both of them. The guy was planning to write off his expenses. He'd kept all his receipts. The girl corroborated his statement. They're both clean, no doubt about it at all."

"Why did Lister kill his daughter? Was there any explanation in the note?"

"The girl was a fornicator and a sinner, a dreadful abomination in the eyes of the Lord." Rossiter sighed theatrically. "Why didn't we think of that in the first place, Jack? We could've solved the damn case the same day you found the body."

"Tell me something," said Willows. "Did Lister mention any other names?"

"You think he might've sliced up the kid in the van?"

"It's a possibility."

"Solve your case for you, wouldn't it?" said Rossiter cynically.

"Say hello to Katie for me," said Willows, and hung up.

"What was that all about?" said Parker.

Willows told her about Lister's suicide and the note he'd left behind.

"Somebody who works in a service station," said Parker

168

thoughtfully, "would know how to hot-wire a car. Or an Econoline van." She frowned. "Maybe Lister thought the kid was pimping for his daughter, got her involved in the business."

"Could be," said Willows. "But I'd say Bill Lister was about fifty years old, and that he looked every minute of it. The man we're after is only about thirty."

"According to that old Chinese woman we talked to. But she must be in her eighties. Who knows what kind of shape her eyes are in."

Willows nodded. He'd been thinking along similar lines. The old lady had impressed him, but what if she'd been wrong?

"Are you going to tell Bradley about this?" said Parker.

"What do you think?"

"I think we should give Spears and Orwell the first shift. We can take over after dinner, watch the Trans Am until whoever's living at Greenbriar Lane packs it in for the night."

There was a Block Brothers "For Sale" sign in front of a large mock Tudor house diagonally across the street from Misha Yokóte's sprawling L-shaped rancher. Eddy Orwell parked the unmarked police car in the driveway, which was hidden from the street by a dense hedge of dwarf cedars. Farley Spears unbuckled his seat belt. He climbed out of the car and went over to the house, pressed his nose against a window and came away smiling.

"It's empty. No furniture, nothing."

"Perfect," said Orwell, reaching for the Zeiss 7x50's on the seat beside him.

The rancher was white, with dark green trim. There was about a hundred and fifty feet of frontage, all gently sloping lawn. The driveway curved up the left side of the property and disappeared into an attached double garage. The garage door wasn't completely down, and with the aid of the binoculars, Spears was able to see the licence plate of the car parked inside. The plate number was identical to the number on the parking ticket issued by Judith Lundstrom.

Spears lit a cigarette. Orwell glared at him, but didn't say anything. Orwell was a vice cop working on a homicide investigation, and he knew he had to watch his step. Spears was a jerk, but what Spears said to Bradley could have a serious impact on Orwell's career. He moved upwind of Spears, and Spears smiled at him, smoke dribbling out of his mouth and nostrils.

Orwell found another gap in the trees and scanned the front of the house. Heavy curtains had been pulled across the windows, either for privacy or to keep out the heat of the afternoon sun. Orwell fine-tuned the binoculars until he could make out the warp and woof of the fabric. It didn't help much.

Farley Spears finished his cigarette and lit another one.

The house shimmered in the heat.

Spears looked down at the city, ten or more miles away and lost in a poisonous grey haze. "I wonder how much it costs to live up here," he said.

"Lots," said Orwell.

"That much, huh." Spears dropped the butt of his cigarette on the asphalt and ground it under his heel. Orwell had a real talent for small talk. It was going to be a long afternoon.

There was a garden tap sticking out of the house to the left of the front door, just above ground level. Spears knelt and turned the handle. The tap made a gurgling sound and a single drop of lukewarm water fell into his cupped hand. He turned the tap off. Smoking dried him out, but he was wired, he couldn't quit. He glanced at Orwell. They only had one pair of binoculars and it was clear that Orwell wasn't about to give them up. He went over to the car and sat down and lit his third cigarette in twenty minutes.

At half-past four, Farley Spears decided to relieve his boredom by taking a short walk. He'd noticed that there was an almost perpendicular wall of rock behind the rancher, about a hundred feet away from the house. The rock wall was at least fifty feet high, topped with a mix of dense shrubbery and stunted evergreens. If he could manage to get up there, he'd have a great view of the fenced back yard, maybe even be able to see inside the house.

"Maybe even fall and break your neck," said Orwell when Spears told him where he was going.

Spears walked up Greenbriar Lane until he was out of sight of the rancher, then cut through somebody's yard and followed a split rail fence up the flank of the cliff. Within a few minutes he was breathing heavily, winded. He paused, and loosened his tie. The air smelled of resin. Insects buzzed wearily past. Spears looked around. He was all alone. He unzipped his trousers and urinated against a cedar fence post, aiming at an ant but missing. When he was finished, he started up the hill again, climbing slowly but steadily, pacing himself.

Ten minutes after he'd left Orwell, Spears was feeling anything but bored. Squatting in the bushes at the top of the cliff, he looked down on a heart-shaped pool, a barbecue full of dead ashes, and a man and a woman making love in the middle of a tiled patio, their dark bodies reflected in a wind-break of glass blocks.

The woman was lying on her back. Spears could see her face. She was Japanese.

"Pleasure to meet you, Miss Yokóte," he said softly.

Inside the house, a telephone warbled.

The man continued his steady rhythm. The woman's hands slid down his back. She gripped his buttocks and squeezed hard. Spears watched the index finger of her right hand disappear between her partner's cheeks. The man began to move a little faster. The telephone warbled musically. Sweat glistened on the man's back. Misha Yokóte slowly lifted her arm, withdrawing three feet of gaily coloured silk scarf from the man's anus. Spears's mouth gaped open. The man bucked and lurched. His knees thumped on the tiles. He cried out, and Misha laughed.

The man rolled off her, on to the hot tiles of the patio. He still had an erection. Spears saw to his surprise that he wasn't Japanese at all, but that he had a very deep tan, that he was tanned all over, every last inch of him.

The telephone hadn't quit. Misha jumped lithely to her feet and padded into the house.

No visible scars, thought Spears. Terrific legs. The phone had stopped ringing. His thigh muscles ached. He shifted his stance and a handful of pebbles rattled down the slope and fell to the narrow strip of lawn between the face of the cliff and the pool.

Misha came out of the house and said, "It's Felix. He wants to talk to you."

Junior nodded. He scratched his groin and strolled into the house.

Spears watched Misha walk along the edge of the pool towards him, climb up on the diving-board and test the spring of it. She stood in profile, perfectly still, as if listening. Spears stared at her breasts. She flexed her knees and began to work the board, got some altitude and arced cleanly beneath the flat pink surface of the water.

Spears' foot dislodged a few more stones, larger ones this time. He was too busy watching Misha to notice.

32

Junior was watching Misha too, as he picked up the telephone.

"Hi, Felix. What's happening?"

"You tell me," Felix snarled right back.

Junior wondered if Misha'd answered the phone with that soft and lazy post-coital voice she liked so much to use. He turned his back on the pool, giving Felix all of his attention. "Well," he said, "I got up about ten, swam a few laps and had some breakfast. Spent maybe an hour washing and waxing the car. Took a shower and watched part of an old John Wayne movie on the TV."

Felix was breathing hard. "Is that it, Junior, or are you saving the best part for last?"

"Thought I might get around to mowing the lawn this afternoon, if it cools down a little."

"Leading a pretty quiet life, are you?"

"You could hear a bullet drop."

"How's Misha?"

"She's okay."

"Voice sounded a little throaty, like she might be coming down with a cold."

"No, she's fine."

"I don't like it," said Felix. "Mannie should've called by now."

"I drove by his place a couple of times last night," said Junior. "His car was parked outside, but he wasn't showing any lights."

"Something's gone wrong, I know it."

"Why the hell you ever hire the guy, if you don't mind me asking."

"I owed his father a favour."

"Oh yeah?"

"It happened long ago, Junior. Before your time."

Junior found that sometime during the conversation he'd

turned so he was facing the pool again. Misha was jumping up and down on the diving-board. She saw him watching, and waved.

"You want me to go back, take a look around, kick his door in?"

"I don't know what I want." He sighed heavily into Junior's ear. "You get Misha on the next plane out of there, okay? Tell her I miss her, tell her anything you want. Just get her packed and on her way."

"Whatever you say, Felix."

"As for Mannie, maybe you ought to hang in there a little longer. Give him some room."

"He ain't gonna phone," said Junior flatly. "Not if he fucked up. And he must've fucked up or he would have phoned by now."

"You think so, eh?"

"I'd bet my life on it."

"Don't talk like that," said Felix quickly. "It's bad luck."

"I know the guy, " said Junior. "He's gonna spend the next six months sitting in his crummy little house, hoping we forgot about him. But we can't afford to do that, can we Felix?"

"I guess not," said Felix slowly. "I hate to admit it, but you're right. He's a liability."

Junior felt a tingle of anticipation. He started making plans, his brain awhirl.

"Be careful," said Felix. "And when you're finished with him, take a minute to look around. Make sure he didn't leave a love note to his lawyer tucked away in the sugar bowl, you know what I mean?"

"Sure," said Junior.

"I hope so," said Felix. He hung up without saying goodbye, but Junior wasn't offended. It was a style thing, was all. Nothing personal. He put the phone down and went back outside, into the sunlight and the heat. He jogged across the patio, dived into the pool and kicked hard, touched bottom and came up on the far side.

Misha was sitting sideways on the board, painted toenails dabbling at the water. She smiled down at him and said, "What did Felix want?"

"He wanted me to make up his mind for him."

"About what?"

"Mannie Katz."

"Really? What'd you decide?"

"Time to say goodbye."

"No wonder you look so sad," Misha joked.

Junior reached up and pulled her shrieking and giggling into the water. He held her close, so their faces were only inches apart. "The reason I'm sad is because you didn't come," he said.

"I never do," she said. "And I never will."

"But why not?"

"Because I couldn't handle the guilt, that's why."

Junior wanted her to try to explain it to him, even though he doubted he'd ever understand. Misha saw the questions coming, deflected them by putting her smooth brown arms around him and kissing him on the mouth.

Junior pulled away, but not too far. "Felix wants you on the next flight out of town," he said.

Misha kissed him again. Her lips tasted faintly of chlorine.

One for the road, thought Junior.

33

Junior got into the car, slammed the door shut. He put the key in the ignition and turned it part-way, so the dashboard lights came on, phosphorescent and green. The quartz clock said fifteen minutes to ten. Five hours ago he'd driven Misha out to the airport, and he could still smell the scent of her perfume, musky and warm. At the terminal she'd treated him like a fucking taxi-driver. Got out of the car without a word and just walked away, hips swinging. Not waving or even bothering to turn at the wide glass doors to take a last, lingering look.

Well, fuck it.

Junior punched the orange button on the remote and the garage door swung open. He put the remote device back in the glove compartment, wedging it under his Colt revolver. Started the engine, drove slowly down the slope of the driveway, turned right on Greenbriar and goosed it.

The city lay far below him, millions of individual lights conspiring to turn the night sky a sickly whitish colour, like the underbelly of a dead fish. Junior had no time for the view, however. He was driving hard, with all the skill and nerve he could muster, his eyes on the blur of asphalt and the red needle of the tachometer. At Southborough he made a left without signalling, taking the corner in a controlled drift that left curving black smears of rubber on the road. It was crazy, driving like this with murder on the agenda and an unregistered and totally illegal handgun in the car. But Junior was frustrated, in a real bad mood, and he knew it was crucial that he get everything out of his system and cool right down before he took on Mannie Katz. The guy had at least a couple of notches on his belt; Junior had to take him seriously.

He passed under the Trans Canada Highway, sound of the twin exhausts bouncing off tons of dull grey pre-form concrete.

Why had Felix wanted Misha back in California? What was the big rush? The man had a nose on him like a bloodhound, was there something in the air Junior didn't get a whiff of? No, probably all that happened was Felix took a little nap and woke up and rolled over, found there was nobody in bed but him. He was lonely, that was all. His bones were cold. If anything serious had gone wrong, Junior'd have been the first to know about it. At least that's what he told himself, and believed, as he turned left off Taylor Way on to Marine Drive and the approach to the Lions Gate bridge.

In the middle of the bridge, stalled in traffic, he thought about how he was going to kill Mannie. Park on the street right in front of the house, so the guy wouldn't get the idea Junior was sneaking up on him. Use the car telephone, tell him what? That Felix was worried and wanted to know what the hell was going on. Did he take care of Carly, grab the videotape? Mow him down with questions, confuse him, keep him off-balance.

No, fuck that. Keep it simple. Just park and walk right up to the house, get inside. Then what? Pull the Colt and let him have it. Fast. No speeches, no getting cute, no fooling around. Mannie was quick as a snake with those knives of his. Fucking cutlery department on wheels. Don't give him a chance. Just stick the front sight in his stomach and bang away. Knock some low-grade hamburger patties off him.

Junior smiled, seeing the look of shock in Mannie's watery blue eyes, feeling the kick of the gun, hearing the explosions, watching him go down.

The traffic started moving again, a slow crawl. He pushed a Lionel Ritchie tape into the deck, turned the sound right up and leant back in his seat. His rear view mirror was full of lights. He had no way of seeing the chocolate-brown Ford Fairlane keeping pace three cars behind him.

34

It was two minutes to ten when Willows heard the faint drone of the garage door motor. He saw the backup lights of the Trans Am flash on, and sprinted for the Fairlane. The starter was grinding away, Parker muttering under her breath as she twisted the key. He jumped inside the car and slammed shut the door. The engine caught, faltered, steadied. They pulled out of the driveway and started down Greenbriar. Two blocks below them, the Trans Am's brake lights vanished around a corner.

Parker turned on her headlights.

"He turned left," said Willows. He fastened his seat-belt.

"Wherever he's going, he sure is in a hurry."

"Let's not lose him."

"Do you want to drive?" said Parker.

"No, you're doing fine."

"Thank you."

The close-set eyes of an animal standing by the side of the road glared bright red. A German Shepherd, black and tan. Parker'd had a Shepherd once, when she was a kid. Sheba. The dog had bitten the milkman when he'd yelled at her mother about an overdue bill, and from then on they'd bought their dairy products at the local Safeway. Parker remembered missing the glass bottles.

"Did you get a look at him?" Willows said.

Parker shook her head, no. The darkness, the Trans Am's tinted windows. She hadn't caught so much as a glimpse of whoever was behind the wheel.

Southborough Drive. Vast expanses of manicured lawn, flowering shrubs that masked the stink of chlorine from the big Olympic-sized pools. The Capilano Golf and Country Club over on the left, the greens and fairways dark and deserted.

They followed Junior down the asphalt-encrusted slope of the mountain, over the Lions Gate bridge and its necklace of lights, along the winding three-lane causeway that bisected the thousand acres of Stanley Park. Past Lost Lagoon and its gaudy illuminated fountain. Parker stayed on Junior's tail as he made his way through the downtown core, down the Mall and over the Granville Street Bridge and straight up Granville to King Edward, east past Cambie, south on Ontario. Willows looked at his watch. It was twenty-five minutes to eleven. They'd been driving for a little over half an hour. Junior had averaged about forty miles an hour, but had hit seventy and eighty in the stretches, weaving in and out of traffic like a madman. At first they thought he knew he was being followed, but after a little while they began to realize it was just the way he liked to drive, with reckless abandon.

The Trans Am turned left on East 30th. The street was flat and narrow, hemmed in on both sides by modest one-storey stucco houses. Nat Bailey stadium was less than a block away; there was a baseball game on and the streets were jammed with cars.

Parker tapped the brake pedal. The Fairlane crept slowly through the intersection. "If I get too close, he's going to spot us. But if I stay too far back, we could lose him."

"Use the lane," said Willows.

Parker drove past 30th and turned down a gravel lane. She turned off the Fairlane's headlights. The car bounced from one pothole to the next, past crumbling garages, abandoned appliances, shapeless piles of junk, rotting mattresses.

"He's slowing down."

Willows nodded. In the narrow gaps between the houses he was able to follow the progress of the Trans Am as it cruised along on a course parallel to their own.

"He stopped."

"Circle around and move in on him," said Willows. He picked up the Phillips microphone and called 312 Main for a back-up.

Parker accelerated through the potholes towards the far end of the block. She swung left on James Street and then left again on 30th. The Trans Am was parked in front of a small brown house with a scruffy front yard and a white picket fence that had been smashed flat. Parker waited until they were about fifty feet away and then turned on her brights, washing the interior of the Trans Am in light.

Junior had the air-conditioner on full. The blast of processed air across the dashboard made the jumble of paper animals vibrate frantically. He squinted and shielded his eyes with his hand as the car moving slowly towards him suddenly crossed to the wrong side of the road and flashed its brights. It occurred to him that Mannie might have been waiting for him, expecting him, that the sneaky son of a bitch had set him up. He flipped open the glove compartment, grabbed his big Colt .357 Magnum.

Parker stopped the Fairlane thirty feet away from the Trans Am. She put the transmission in Park.

Willows saw the Trans Am's door swing open, a man step out of the car. He was at least six foot tall, muscular, heavily tanned. There was no resemblance at all to the description given by the elderly Chinese woman from the grocery store. He reached for the mike to call off the back-up.

Junior thumbed back the hammer of the Colt. He brought his right arm up, bisected Parker's forehead with the blade front sight and calmly squeezed the trigger. The gun bucked in his hand and the rear window of the Fairlane blew out. Both doors swung open. Junior got off a second shot. He had an idea he was shooting wild, but how the hell was he supposed to correct when he didn't know where the fuck his rounds were going? Night shooting was a bitch. He'd have to look into it, see if he could get his hands on some tracers.

Willows fired three times as quickly as he could pull the trigger, not taking the time to aim properly, simply returning fire. All three shots hit the Trans Am's radiator, the standard-issue 358 grain wadcutters fragmenting on impact. A triangular chunk of copper jacketing sliced through the Trans Am's fuel line an inch from the pump. High octane gasoline spurted across the engine block, dribbled down on the manifold.

Parker had bailed out of the Fairlane, using her open door for cover. "Police!" she shouted. "Drop your weapon and put your hands on your head!"

Junior aimed at the car door and fired twice. The Fairlane's windscreen turned frosty white. He cocked the gun and turned his attention back to the other cop, the shooter.

The gasoline puddling on the manifold finally ignited. There was a searing flare of orange, an explosion that rattled windows up and down the block. The bonnet of the Trans Am spiralled straight up into the air on a column of smoke and flame.

Parker, lying on her stomach on the road, aimed and fired.

The bullet sent Junior spinning sideways into the car. The sleeve of his shirt caught fire. There was blood on his chest. He dropped the Colt and fell to his knees. He could smell something burning. His hair.

Willows sensed a movement to his left. A man wearing tan slacks and a pale green or blue polo shirt was standing uncertainly on the front porch of the house with the ruined picket fence. Willows had never seen the man before, but he recognized him instantly. He started across the road towards the sidewalk and Mannie ran for it, scooting around the side of the house into darkness. Willows glanced behind him. Parker was moving cautiously in on Junior, a fire-extinguisher in her left hand, her revolver in her right. Junior was rolling around on the asphalt, screaming.

Willows went after Mannie.

Mannie had run into darkness and now he was running towards the lights and noise of the stadium. He reached the end of the lane and cut diagonally across Ontario towards the gravel parking lot at the rear of the stadium. His first thought had been to slip inside, do some mingling. Buy himself a hot dog and a paper cup of beer and kind of blend in with the fans. But as he trotted towards the empty turnstiles he realized that the stadium, brightly lit and easily sealed off, was a trap. Veering away from the entrance, he made his way through the ranks of parked cars on a zig-zag route that would take him into the deep shadow of the right field fence, cover him all the way to centre field, where he could cross Midlothian Avenue into Queen Elizabeth Park.

The park was a hundred acres, more or less, and it was shaped roughly like a huge ear. There was a lot of open, grassy area, and a network of access roads. But there was also plenty of natural cover – broken ground, stands of deciduous trees, dense thickets of shrubbery.

Mannie sank to his hands and knees in the shadow of a rusty

Buick station wagon. He was breathing hard through his mouth and there was a stitch in his side, hot and sharp. He rested for a moment and then stood up, crouching, and risked a quick look behind him. The cop was about two hundred feet away, standing on the roof of a pickup truck. His back was to Mannie. He started to turn around and Mannie ducked down, his heart beating against his ribs like a tightly clenched fist. They'd give him twenty-five years for the kid and another quarter-century for the gorilla in the Jockey shorts, who'd tried to kill him with the fridge. It was too much fucking time and Mannie knew he wouldn't be able to handle it, he'd go crazy. He scuttled towards the fence, gravel crunching under his shoes and digging into the palms of his hands. There were sirens everywhere, faint but unmistakable, converging on him from every point of the compass. If he was going to get out of this mess that Junior had laid on him, he'd to move fast, make no mistakes.

Standing on the roof of the truck, Willows saw Mannie bolt from the cover of the parking lot across thirty feet of open ground, his elongated shadow chasing him into the deeper shadow cast by the stadium fence. Mannie had committed himself. He was heading for the park. Given his limited options, it wasn't all that bad a choice. Willows wondered how Parker was doing, if she'd thought to call the dog squad. He jumped down from the truck and started to jog through the field of empty cars. As he ran, he studied the general layout of the park. To his left, there was an open, gently sloping grassy area. To the right a narrow strip of thick brush meandered down the hill towards several small ponds, more grass, patches of shrubbery, brush. The park was all hillside. At the top there was a domed arboretum and, if he remembered correctly, a natural depression about fifty feet deep and several hundred feet wide, the bottom planted in grass and flowers.

Willows had just reached the edge of the parking lot when Mannie suddenly bolted from the cover of the fence, across the road and into the park. A dim, indistinct shape, he ran straight up the middle of the open area and then turned sharply right, plunged into the strip of brush and came out the other side, running towards the ponds.

He couldn't be sure, but Willows thought he knew what Mannie would do next. He followed Mannie across Midlothian

Avenue and up the slope. The grass was heavy with dew; it was easy to see where Mannie had gone off to the right. Instead of veering after him, Willows kept going straight up the hill, keeping on a course parallel to the thick strip of brush. As he'd guessed, the brush marked the course of a shallow ravine, a depression formed over the years by rainwater draining down into the ponds. Willows kept low, but made no real attempt at concealment. Either Mannie would see him or he wouldn't. It was a question of timing, and of luck.

He continued up the slope, pacing himself, going as fast as he could without losing his wind.

Mannie leaned against a stunted cherry tree growing near the bank of a small pond. His legs were trembling with fatigue. His lungs were on fire. Too many nights spent in front of the TV, gobbling junk food and drinking beer. He was going to have to buy one of those designer jogging outfits, start getting up a little earlier, do a few laps around the neighbourhood every morning before hitting the granola.

A car drove slowly past, headlights sweeping across the black surface of the water and beyond, to a wide expanse of mowed grass. Mannie saw he'd made a mistake, taken a wrong turn somewhere. He was exactly where he didn't want to be, out in the open, exposed and vulnerable. Another car cruised past. A face, pale and inquisitive, peered out the side window. Mannie didn't know if he'd been seen or not.

He ran back to the cover of the ravine and scrambled blindly upwards, slipped and fell, banged a knee. The floor of the ravine was littered with broken shale, the fragments thin and sharp. With each step he took, he caused a miniature landslide. He knelt and took off his shoes. Much better. In his stockinged feet he was able to move through the darkness in almost absolute silence, a shadow among shadows.

From his vantage point high up on the hill, Willows could see the sparkling red and blue lights of an ambulance, fire trucks, at least half a dozen patrol cars. Plenty of men and equipment down there, but it seemed nobody had thought to come and lend him a hand. He was sure now that Claire Parker hadn't seen him go after Mannie. He wondered if there was a car from the dog squad down there, how long it would take to follow his scent into the park. Then he heard the tin-whistle screech of a disturbed bird, and knew that wherever Rover was, he wasn't going to make it in time for the party.

The sides of the ravine had become increasingly shallow, and now, suddenly, the ravine petered out altogether. Mannie found himself standing on a narrow path that ran diagonally across the slope of the hill, up towards the faint glow of the arboretum. There was a stand of scrawny trees to his left, a clump of rocks off to the right. He started up the path and one of the rocks stood up.

"Police," said Willows softly. "Put your hands up and don't move."

"What?" said Mannie. The way the guy was holding his body, Mannie knew he had a gun. He was also very much aware that he was backlit by the powerful arc lights of the ball park. It was a perfect situation, but not for him. He'd provided the cop with the kind of sharp-edged silhouette target he'd normally only expect to find on a firing-range.

Willows inched closer, his gun extended in front of him in a two-handed grip. "Police," he said again. "Put your hands on top of your head. Do it now."

"Okay," said Mannie. "Whatever you say." He lifted his arms and a tongue of flame leapt up at him, actually reached out and touched him. He felt a searing heat, and was dazzled, blinded by the muzzle flash. At the same instant he heard a sharp report, a thunderclap of sound so loud it hurt his ears. He couldn't believe it. For some reason the dumb fucking cop had fired a warning shot. He stumbled backwards, lost his balance and fell into the mouth of the ravine, slid a few feet and was still. Lying motionless and blind on his bed of stones, he cried out and heard nothing.

He tried to imagine what had happened. His imagination failed him. There was a shift of time. No pain, only silence. Then, gradually, he became aware of the reassuring sound of his heart at work. He focused on the moist thumping of it, the hiss of the valves opening and closing, the rush and thunder of his blood as it was pumped through a network of arteries and veins into the fading depths of his body. As he listened, the rhythm quickened and the noise and clamour intensified until his entire body shook with the power and force of it.

And then, all at once, it stopped.

* * *

184

The narrow beam of a five-cell flashlight played over yellow teeth, pinched nostrils, corroded skin, eyes that were all pupil, black and sightless. Parker knelt down beside Willows, touched him lightly on the shoulder.

"Are you okay, Jack?"

"Better than him."

Parker ran the beam of light across Mannie's pale green polo shirt. Willows had shot Mannie right through the alligator.

"Let's see his hands," said Willows.

Parker focused the spot on Mannie's outflung right hand. A quartet of heavy gold rings caught the light and threw it back at her.

"I thought he had a knife," said Willows. "All he was packing was a handful of jewellery."

"Maybe, and maybe not," said Parker quickly. "If he had a knife, he would have dropped it when you shot him. It could be anywhere. It could be fifty feet down the hill." She squeezed Willows' arm. "Let's get the dogs up here, and some lights and metal detectors, and see what we find, okay?"

Willows stood up. He holstered his revolver. "I'm going home, Claire."

"Is that a good idea? Inspector Bradley's going to want to talk to you."

"It can wait."

Parker hesitated. "I'm going downtown anyway, why don't I give you a ride."

"I'm not going downtown," said Willows. "I'm going home. Back to the wife and kids. If Sheila doesn't like it, *she* can move into the goddam apartment."

There were cops all over the mountain, moving in fast. As soon as Willows turned his back, Claire Parker started running her hands over the corpse. There was a straight razor in the back pocket of the tan slacks. Parker snapped open the blade. She closed Mannie's lifeless fingers around the bone handle and then kicked the razor out of his hand and into the darkness, heard it skitter over the shale. There was a throaty roar from the crowd at Nat Bailey Stadium. A tiny white ball arked high into the air, was lost in the glare of the lights. Parker stood there for a moment, thinking about what she had done. She switched off the flashlight.

Mannie Katz vanished like a bad dream.

The old man still liked a beer now and then. Misha, always looking to score a few extra points, had troubled herself to lug home a case of Labatt's Classic, a premium quality brew she didn't believe was available in southern California. Felix was drinking a bottle now, watching her critically as she fiddled with the TV receiver, trying to get the dish up on the roof to suck CBC Vancouver down out of the heavens.

Felix didn't say a word as she fumbled with the controls, but she could hear his raspy impatient breathing, feel his lizard eyes on the nape of her neck.

Eventually a woman with thick auburn hair and gelled lips snapped into focus on the Sony's twenty-eight inch screen.

"That's it," said Felix. "Hold it right there."

Misha turned and gave him a smile that was meant to be reassuring. Felix had been drinking all evening. Wine with dinner, shot glasses of Glenlivet afterwards, then the beer. He was long past the point of simply being drunk. He was also nervous and irritable, growing increasingly worried about Junior. Misha was worried too. Junior should've phoned as soon as he'd dealt with the problem that was Mannie Katz. Called out of common courtesy, if nothing else. He was supposed to give Felix a ring whenever he did anything even remotely dangerous, never mind attempting to murder a professional killer. If something had gone wrong in Vancouver, Misha would catch the flak. And there'd be a lot of it, for sure. She moved away from the TV, careful to keep out of Felix's line of sight.

Felix brusquely patted the chesterfield. "Come on over here and sit down, will you."

They watched several minutes' coverage of a children's fishing derby in False Creek. Ranks of beaming toddlers proudly displayed a variety of tiny dead fish that had been yanked from the sea. Felix drank beer and held Misha's hand.

She could feel his fingernails, blunt and prehensile, digging into her palm.

The woman with the auburn hair came back on the screen. She looked serious.

Misha had a sense of impending doom. She found herself standing at a shot of the burnt-out hulk of a car. The fire had burned so hot that there was nothing left but the body and engine and frame, a few large unidentifiable chunks of metal.

"What the hell's all this about?" Felix said.

The camera panned out on to the street. There was something rectangular and black about halfway up the block. The camera zoomed in. The black object turned out to be the crumpled bonnet of a Pontiac Trans Am. Felix recognized it by the big sprawled-out gold eagle painted on it.

"Oh my God," he said.

There was a quick cut to a couple of white-coated ambulance attendants easing a bagged corpse into the back of an ambulance. Lights flashing, blue and red. Mannie Katz's name was mentioned, voice-over. Felix hardly heard a word that was said, his heart was beating so loudly.

There was an establishing shot of a hospital, then a long shot of a cop sitting in a wooden chair at the end of a brightly lit corridor with bare walls and a polished linoleum floor. Felix pushed himself up off the chesterfield and went over and turned up the sound. His son Junior Newton was in the intensive care ward with a bullet wound in his chest and second and third degree burns all down the left side of his body, unknown internal injuries. His condition was critical.

Felix hurled the bottle of Labatt's Classic at the TV screen. It bounced off the thick glass and fell to the carpet spewing foam. Felix kicked the bottle across the room and went outside, on to the porch that fronted the house. He left the door wide-open behind him. The beach was easily a hundred yards away, but there was an offshore wind and the ocean was noisy. Misha could hear the waves slamming down on the hard-packed sand, the dull grinding of stones caught in the surf. She went over to the door and looked out. Felix was curled up in a wicker chair at the far end of the porch, his hands clenched in his lap. In the orange glow of the bug lights she could see his chest rising and falling spasmodically, tears of grief and rage spilling down his withered cheeks. He must have sensed her presence, because after a moment he looked up, glaring at her with bloodshot eyes.

"I want my boy back," he said, his voice thick with sorrow. He coughed, teeth flashing a dull orange. "I don't care how much it costs, just do it."

"Yes," said Misha.

"Wait for me upstairs," said Felix.

Nodding, Misha stepped quickly back inside the house. Although she knew Felix very well, she'd never before seen him express any emotion but anger. Now they had shared a moment of compassion, human distress. And she was frightened. A man like Felix, once you had discovered his weakness, would feel he had no choice but to display his strength.

She stooped to pick up the beer bottle Felix had thrown at the television. As her fingers touched the curved surface of the glass a thought occurred to her; an idea that came uninvited but was nevertheless warmly received.

Junior had tried to shoot a policeman and was a suspect in a murder investigation. He was a foreigner, as well. How high would his bail be set, once he was capable of leaving the hospital? Misha tried to imagine it. A hundred thousand dollars, easily. Perhaps as much as half a million, who could say! There was a joke Junior made the day Felix bought the Laguna Beach house. That Felix needed so many bedrooms because where else would he keep all his money if not stuffed inside his mattresses. This was an exaggeration, of course, but grounded in truth. Felix did have a tendency to keep his assets liquid. The more she thought about it the surer she was that he'd give her cash to take care of the Canadian courts. A suitcase crammed with small bills, perhaps a week's profit from his various enterprises.

A woman could go anywhere in the world with a hundred thousand dollars. She could even visit Japan, if she liked.

Misha forced herself to be calm, to concern herself with realities rather than dreams. She listened to the waves pound the beach and to the abrasive thunder of stones imprisoned in the surf; to the sounds of America's coastline chewing itself to pieces. Certified cheques weren't Felix's style. To his way of thinking a piece of paper was worthless unless it had the face of a president engraved on it. She considered Tokyo. In Tokyo or any other large city in Japan there would be many opportunities for a woman of her varied tastes, unusual talents. It would be easy to change her appearance; to let her hair grow down to her hips, wear the clothes of her ancestors, learn once again to think and speak only in the language of her childhood. Felix might very well summon up the energy to go after her, but who would he chase? How could he hope to find a woman he had never really known and who in any case had ceased to exist?

Misha giggled. Windchimes. The twittering of glass sparrows. She covered her face with her hands, revelled in the touch of lacquered nails on skin.

Out on the porch, under the bug lights, Felix sat hunched in his wicker chair and stared out at the blackness of the night, the uncertain, crumbling, chalk-white demarcation line of the surf.

He'd already run out of tears. There was a lot to think about, and he was thinking hard.

FOR THE BEST IN PAPERBACKS, LOOK FOR THE

In every corner of the world, on every subject under the sun, Penguin represents quality and variety—the very best in publishing today.

For complete information about books available from Penguin—including Pelicans, Puffins, Peregrines, and Penguin Classics—and how to order them, write to us at the appropriate address below. Please note that for copyright reasons the selection of books varies from country to country.

In the United Kingdom: For a complete list of books available from Penguin in the U.K., please write to *Dept E.P., Penguin Books Ltd, Harmondsworth, Middlesex, UB7 0DA.*

In the United States: For a complete list of books available from Penguin in the U.S., please write to *Dept BA, Penguin*, Box 999, Bergenfield, New Jersey 07621-0999.

In Canada: For a complete list of books available from Penguin in Canada, please write to *Penguin Books Canada Ltd, 2801 John Street, Markham, Ontario L3R 1B4.*

In Australia: For a complete list of books available from Penguin in Australia, please write to the *Marketing Department, Penguin Books Australia Ltd, P.O. Box 257, Ringwood, Victoria 3134.*

In New Zealand: For a complete list of books available from Penguin in New Zealand, please write to the *Marketing Department, Penguin Books (NZ) Ltd, Private Bag, Takapuna, Auckland 9.*

In India: For a complete list of books available from Penguin, please write to *Penguin Overseas Ltd, 706 Eros Apartments, 56 Nehru Place, New Delhi, 110019.*

In Holland: For a complete list of books available from Penguin in Holland, please write to *Penguin Books Nederland B.V., Postbus 195, NL–1380AD Weesp, Netherlands.*

In Germany: For a complete list of books available from Penguin, please write to *Penguin Books Ltd, Friedrichstrasse 10–12, D–6000 Frankfurt Main 1, Federal Republic of Germany.*

In Spain: For a complete list of books available from Penguin in Spain, please write to *Longman Penguin España, Calle San Nicolas 15, E–28013 Madrid, Spain.*

In Japan: For a complete list of books available from Penguin in Japan, please write to *Longman Penguin Japan Co Ltd, Yamaguchi Building, 2-12-9 Kanda Jimbocho, Chiyuoda-Ku, Tokyo 101, Japan.*